HER CONSIGLIERE

Praise for Carsen Taite

Spirit of the Law

"I would definitely recommend this to romance fans and those that like their romance to include lawyers and a little bit of mystery. Due to the slight paranormal elements I think paranormal romance fans would also enjoy this even if they don't normally read Taite."
—*LGBTQ Reader*

Best Practice

"I had fun reading this story and watching the final law partner find her true love. If you like a delightful, romantic age-gap tale involving lawyers, you will like *Best Practice*. In fact, I believe you will like all three books in the Legal Affairs series."—*Rainbow Reflections*

"I think this could very well be my favourite book in this series. *Best Practice* is a light and easy opposites-attract age-gap read. It's well-paced and fun, not overly angsty, with just enough tension to be exciting."—*Jude in the Stars*

Drawn

"This book held my attention from start to finish. I'm a huge Taite fan and I love it when she writes lesbian crime romance books. Because Taite knows so much about the law, it gives her books an authentic feel that I love…Ms. Taite builds the relationship between the main characters with a strong bond and excellent chemistry. Both characters are opposites in many ways but their attraction is undeniable and sizzling."—*LezReviewBooks.com*

Out of Practice

"Taite combines legal and relationship drama to create this realistic and deeply enjoyable lesbian romance…The reliably engaging Taite neatly balances romance and red-hot passion with a plausible legal story line, well-drawn characters, and pitch-perfect pacing that culminates in the requisite heartfelt happily-ever-after."
—*Publishers Weekly*

"[A] quick read romance that gave me all the good feelings. I recommend to people who like to read about romance, vacations, flings, lawyers, blogging, weddings, friends, fighting the feelings, grand gestures, protesters, and wedding veils."—*Bookvark*

Leading the Witness

"This was an enjoyable read. I recommend this to those who like mystery, suspense, prosecution, investigations, romance, and Balcones bourbon."—*Bookvark*

Practice Makes Perfect

"This book has two fantastic leads, an attention-grabbing plot and that sizzling chemistry that great authors can make jump off the page. While all of Taite's books are fantastic, this one is on that next level. This is a damn good book and I cannot wait to see what is next in this series."—*Romantic Reader Blog*

Pursuit of Happiness

"I like Taite's style of writing. She is consistent in terms of quality and always writes strong female characters that are as intelligent as they are beautiful."—*Lesbian Reading Room*

"I can't believe I'm saying this, but I think Meredith and Stevie are my new favourite couple that Taite's written…They're brilliant, funny, and the chemistry between them is out of control."—*Lesbian Review*

Love's Verdict

"Carsen Taite excels at writing legal thrillers with lesbian main characters using her experience as a criminal defense attorney." —*Lez Review Books*

Outside the Law

"[A] fabulous closing to the Lone Star Law series…Tanner and Sydney's journey back to each other is sweet, sexy and sure to keep you entertained."—*Romantic Reader Blog*

A More Perfect Union

"Readers looking for a mix of intrigue and romance set against a political backdrop will want to pick up Taite's latest novel."
—*RT Book Reviews*

"A sexy soldier...Yes, please!!!...Character chemistry was excellent, and I think with such an intricate background story going on, it was remarkable that Carsen Taite didn't lose the characters' romance in that and still kept it at the front and centre of the storyline."
—*Les Rêveur*

Sidebar

"*Sidebar* is a sexy, fun, interesting book that's sure to delight, whether you're a longtime fan or this is your first time reading something by Carsen Taite. I definitely recommend it!"—*Lesbian Review*

Letter of the Law

"Fiery clashes and lots of chemistry, you betcha!"—*Romantic Reader Blog*

Without Justice

"Another pretty awesome lesbian mystery thriller by Carsen Taite."
—*Danielle Kimerer, Librarian, Nevins Memorial Library (MA)*

"All in all a fantastic novel...Unequivocally 5 Stars."—*Les Rêveur*

Above the Law

"[R]eaders who enjoyed the first installment will find this a worthy second act."—*Publishers Weekly*

"Ms. Taite delivered and then some, all the while adding more questions...I like the mystery and intrigue in this story. It has many 'sit on the edge of your seat' scenes of excitement and dread...and drama...well done indeed!"—*Prism Book Alliance*

Reasonable Doubt

"Another Carsen Taite novel that kept me on the edge of my seat… [A]n interesting plot with lots of mystery and a bit of thriller as well. The characters were great."—*Danielle Kimerer, Librarian, Reading Public Library*

Lay Down the Law

"Recognized for the pithy realism of her characters and settings drawn from a Texas legal milieu, Taite pays homage to the prime-time soap opera *Dallas* in pairing a cartel-busting U.S. attorney, Peyton Davis, with a charity-minded oil heiress, Lily Gantry." —*Publishers Weekly*

"Suspenseful, intriguingly tense, and with a great developing love story, this book is delightfully solid on all fronts."—*Rainbow Book Reviews*

Courtship

"Taite (*Switchblade*) keeps the stakes high as two beautiful and brilliant women fueled by professional ambitions face daunting emotional choices…As backroom politics, secrets, betrayals, and threats race to be resolved without political damage to the president, the cat-and-mouse relationship game between Addison and Julia has the reader rooting for them. Taite prolongs the fever-pitch tension to the final pages. This pleasant read with intelligent heroines, snappy dialogue, and political suspense will satisfy Taite's devoted fans and new readers alike."—*Publishers Weekly*

Switchblade

"Dallas's intrepid female bounty hunter, Luca Bennett, is back in another adventure. Fantastic! Between her many friends and lovers, her interesting family, her fly by the seat of her pants lifestyle, and a whole host of detractors there is rarely a dull moment." —*Rainbow Book Reviews*

Beyond Innocence

"Taite keeps you guessing with delicious delay until the very last minute...Taite's time in the courtroom lends *Beyond Innocence* a terrific verisimilitude someone not in the profession couldn't impart. And damned if she doesn't make practicing law interesting." —*Out in Print*

The Best Defense

"Real-life defense attorney Carsen Taite polishes her fifth work of lesbian fiction, *The Best Defense*, with the realism she daily encounters in the office and in the courts. And that polish is something that makes *The Best Defense* shine as an excellent read." —*Out & About Newspaper*

Nothing but the Truth

"Author Taite is really a Dallas defense attorney herself, and it's obvious her viewpoint adds considerable realism to her story, making it especially riveting as a mystery. I give it four stars out of five."—*Bob Lind, Echo Magazine*

Do Not Disturb

"Taite's tale of sexual tension is entertaining in itself, but a number of secondary characters...add substantial color to romantic inevitability."—*Richard Labonte, Book Marks*

It Should Be a Crime—Lammy Finalist

"Taite, a criminal defense attorney herself, has given her readers a behind the scenes look at what goes on during the days before a trial. Her descriptions of lawyer/client talks, investigations, police procedures, etc. are fascinating. Taite keeps the action moving, her characters clear, and never allows her story to get bogged down in paperwork. *It Should Be a Crime* has a fast-moving plot and some extraordinarily hot sex."—*Just About Write*

By the Author

Truelesbianlove.com

It Should Be a Crime

Do Not Disturb

Nothing but the Truth

The Best Defense

Beyond Innocence

Rush

Courtship

Reasonable Doubt

Without Justice

Sidebar

A More Perfect Union

Love's Verdict

Pursuit of Happiness

Leading the Witness

Drawn

Double Jeopardy (novella in Still Not Over You)

Spirit of the Law

Her Consigliere

The Luca Bennett Mystery Series:

Slingshot

Battle Axe

Switchblade

Bow and Arrow (novella in Girls with Guns)

Lone Star Law Series:

Lay Down the Law	Letter of the Law
Above the Law	Outside the Law

Legal Affairs Romances

Practice Makes Perfect	Best Practice
Out of Practice	

Visit us at www.boldstrokesbooks.com

HER CONSIGLIERE

by
Carsen Taite

2021

HER CONSIGLIERE

ISBN 13: 978-1-63555-924-8

This Trade Paperback Original Is Published By
Bold Strokes Books, Inc.
P.O. Box 249
Valley Falls, NY 12185

First Edition: June 2021

CREDITS
Editor: Cindy Cresap
Production Design: Stacia Seaman
Cover Design by Tammy Seidick

Acknowledgments

Like my pal Ali Vali, I'm a big fan of all the OG mobster books and movies: *The Godfather*, *Goodfellas*, *Donnie Brasco*, just to name a few. So, naturally, when I decided I wanted to write a story set in that world, the first thing I did was call Ali, the undisputed don of lesbian mobsters, to tell her my plan. Like the great friend she is, she cheered me on and offered me a special gift, which you will find within the pages of this book. Molte grazie, Ali! Next time I see you, the old-fashioneds and cannoli are on me.

Thanks to Rad and Sandy and the entire crew at Bold Strokes Books for running the best publishing house in the biz—I'm proud to call BSB home. Huge thanks to my smart, funny, and very patient editor, Cindy Cresap. Tammy, thank you for another striking cover—you get me.

A big shout-out to Georgia for our daily check-ins, which keep me on track and motivated when I'd rather be binge-watching whatever's new on Netflix. Many thanks to Maggie Cummings for patiently answering my endless questions about undercover work—your advice was excellent and any mistakes in the manuscript are all mine. Hugs to Ruth, Melissa, Kris, and Elle—I can't wait until we can all gather in person again. And special thanks to my bestie Paula for reading every draft, brainstorming plot points, and being an amazing friend—always.

Thanks to my wife, Lainey, for always believing in my dreams even when they involve sacrificing our time together. I couldn't live this dream without you and I wouldn't want to.

And to you, dear reader, thank you for taking a chance on my work and coming back for more. Every time you purchase one of my stories, you give me the gift of allowing me to make a living doing what I love. Thanks for taking this journey with me.

To Lainey—my consigliere.

Chapter One

Royal Scott stood with her hands in the air, praying the two guys pointing guns at her chest were more interested in the guns and money she was transporting than killing her. "You guys are making a big mistake. You have no idea who I am," she said, acutely conscious of exactly how much they did not know and praying if she kept their attention focused on her, her cohort, Danny, who was in the back of the truck might be able to get the jump on them.

"We know enough." The burly one closest to her grabbed her hands with one fist and roughly cinched them together with a zip tie, while the other one kept his gun trained on her. In an answer to her prayer, Danny appeared behind them. She resisted calling out to him in order to add to the element of surprise, but she was the one who was surprised when he clapped his hand on the shoulder of the guy with the gun.

"Hey, Eduardo, you have everything under control?"

Eduardo laughed. "Couldn't have been any easier. I thought you said she was one of the tough ones."

"She is, but she's also dumb enough to bite the hand that feeds her and think she can get away with it," Danny replied.

"You should be more careful about the company you keep," Eduardo said, this time his comment directed at Royal.

"Right back at you," she replied. She stared at Danny, who ducked his head under the scrutiny. "What the hell, Danny? You set me up?"

"It's more of a takedown than a setup. I brought you in and you've been trying to take my place for months. It's time you learned who's boss." He gestured at Eduardo and his big friend. "Besides, they offered me way more for this shipment than the Garzas are paying."

"And you think these guys are going to let you walk away after you watch them steal this load?"

Danny shrugged. "We worked something out. You're the one who should be worried. The Garzas know you were the one with the intel about this shipment, not me." He pointed at his chest. "I used to be the top lieutenant until I brought you in, you ungrateful bitch."

The one with the intel. That was her all right, and she realized exactly what was going down. He'd not only given up the information about this shipment, but he'd arranged to give her up as well. She should've anticipated his betrayal since the Garzas had come to favor her over him over the last couple of months. And it wasn't like she held any false sense of loyalty toward Danny, but after spending months ingratiating herself into the upper echelons of the Garza cartel, the lines between friends and enemies had started to blur and she'd lost her edge. Was she going to die in this alley, having accomplished absolutely nothing for all her hard work?

As if in answer to her question, one of the thugs marched her to a nearby van and tossed her in the back. She heard the door shut behind her and the lock slide in place and blinked while her eyes adjusted to the darkness. She needn't have bothered trying to see. The space was empty. No seats, no cargo, nothing. She scrambled to her feet and crouched near the door, trying desperately to hear what the men outside were saying.

"Where should we take her?"

"I know a place," Danny said. "It's out of the way and you'll have no trouble getting her to talk. She knows about the other shipments—you can count on it." The words were chilling, and Royal shuddered.

"I don't care what you do to her," Danny added. "But she can't turn back up alive. If she tells the Garzas what just went down, we'll all be dead."

Again, Royal was struck by the betrayal. How had she let herself become so out of touch that she expected any sort of loyalty from a man who'd spent his entire adult life honing his criminal expertise? When this was over, she needed to examine her ability to read people because she'd made a mess of this situation.

You'll have no trouble getting her to talk? Shit, the only way this was going to be over was with her dead body dumped somewhere in the west Texas desert. Death was always a possibility with these jobs, but she'd had the good fortune to steer clear of danger so far in her career. The idea that she'd lost her edge after almost ten years as an agent caused her to double over with her stomach lurching. She beat her fists against the van door in a panic. She'd been in trouble before, but nothing she hadn't been able to handle. This was different. Even if these guys didn't kill her, the Garzas would put a hit out on her for failing to show up with their shipment. She had to get out of here or she'd die either way.

When the van's engine started, her opportunity to escape narrowed, and she beat against the walls of the van harder still.

"Shut up back there. We're just going for a ride."

Royal slumped against the wall and slid to the floor. How

the hell had she wound up here? She'd been doing undercover work for years and never had she so disastrously misread the situation. She'd had absolutely no idea Danny might be working against her. He was the one who'd brought her into the fold, and she'd made them both lots of money over the course of the last year. She could understand if he felt threatened that she might try to take over his share of the business, but she'd been especially careful to foster her image as the dutiful employee being mentored by his more experienced self no matter how much it chafed her to have to work under a guy she knew wasn't as smart as her. In the beginning, he'd always treated her well, cutting her into jobs he could've kept for himself, and it wasn't until the last couple of months, he'd balked at working with her. She knew the change was because the Garzas had started to favor her over him, but she hadn't tuned in to the depth of his envy. If she didn't figure a way out of this situation fast, she was going to pay the ultimate price for her carelessness.

Noise. With her hands tied and her gun gone, noise was her only weapon, and she made the most of it. She turned so her boots were against the van wall and placed both feet together, repeatedly jamming them against the metal with every ounce of strength she could summon. The van kept moving, but the small sliding door between the passenger compartment and cargo hold opened, and a gruff voice shouted at her to keep it down.

"Fuck off," she yelled.

"Shut her up," Danny snapped at Eduardo. She stared at the still open pass-thru window waiting for one of them to say something more, but all she heard was a grunted reply. She started to resume her noise campaign when an idea flashed in her mind. As quietly as possible, she rolled toward the front right corner of the van and painstakingly worked her legs through her arms so that her hands were in front of her body.

"I don't hear anything anymore. Maybe she passed out."

Royal used the cover of their laughing to wedge her body against the corner and push herself into a crouch. She inched her way toward the window, careful to keep low and out of sight. She waited until the van came to a stop, and then she slammed her hands against the wall and yelled as loud as she could. A second later, a gun barrel appeared above her head, followed by Eduardo's face.

"Shut the fuck up, you crazy bitch!"

She lunged for his wrists, wrestling for control of the gun. He pulled back, but she wasn't about to let this opportunity get away, and she shoved as much of her body as would fit through the open space.

"Get off of me," he grunted.

"Fat chance. Drop the gun."

He answered by pulling the trigger, and the sound of the bullet hitting the back of the van echoed. He looked surprised to have missed and she took advantage of his momentary lapse to grab his neck and begin choking him. His gun hand flailed and he struggled against her grip, barely able to get out the words, "Drive, you idiot. Drive."

Royal heard the squeal of the tires as the van lurched forward at breakneck speed, and her hands started to slip as her feet slid on the metal floor unable to find purchase. She fought to hold on, certain this was her only chance to get away, but the van only accelerated faster.

BOOM. She heard the sound of the impact before she registered feeling it—her ears ringing as her body flew through the air. Her hands were no longer attached to the guy's neck, her entire body no longer attached to anything. Like an astronaut on a spaceship, she cartwheeled through the air, gravity be damned. Except her spaceship—the van—cartwheeled with her, propelling her through the enclosed space in chaotic fashion. Her body shot toward the rear door and she braced for impact, but something wasn't right. She rubbed her eyes, briefly noting a warm, wet sensation, and stared hard, but instead of metal in her path, she saw trees and grass and a man running toward her, yelling words she couldn't make out. Her last thought before she shot out of the back was that this was the first time on the job she hadn't been successful at closing a case, and she'd never have another chance.

Chapter Two

Siobhan Collins leaned back in her chair, waiting for the tirade she knew was coming.

"Our primary witness is missing, and"—AUSA Latham pointed directly at her—"they know where he is."

Siobhan's only reaction was to stand and, in a strong and steady voice, address the judge. "Your Honor, I simply cannot let such a baseless accusation stand," she said, immediately drawing a contrast between her and the foaming at the mouth prosecutor. She was the rational one. The rule-following one. Calm, collected, and confident.

Judge Baker nodded. "Please respond."

"This is the third trial setting. We have been more than patient with the government's requests for more time, but Mr. Girardo wants this matter resolved in order to resume his life. We came to court today, as we have on each of the prior settings, ready to try this case. Perhaps if we begin, the government's witness might decide to reappear in time to testify before they rest their case."

"She knows that's not going to happen," the prosecutor barked. "Permission to voir dire the defendant."

Siobhan didn't bother reacting since she knew there was no way in hell any federal judge was going to let the prosecutor question a defendant who hadn't voluntarily waived his right to testify. And Jimmy Girardo aka Jimmy G wasn't going to be doing anything that stupid. Not while she was his lawyer.

"Permission denied." Judge Baker rubbed the bridge of his nose before looking down it at the AUSA. "Mr. Latham, you will recall that at the last motion hearing, I told you there would be no more continuances. Correct?"

"Yes, Your Honor, but there was no way to anticipate the disappearance of our witness."

Siobhan rolled her eyes. "Your Honor, their primary witness is on parole. The government should know where he is at any given moment. I, for one, as a citizen, find it disturbing that the very people who are supposed to be keeping tabs on this dangerous criminal—their words, not mine," she held up a copy of the police report documenting the witness's crimes, "could lose him, especially on the eve of what the government has been billing as a very important trial. If this trial is important, then they should act like it. We oppose any delay. Our witnesses are ready and waiting."

Judge Baker motioned to his deputy, who handed him a piece of paper. "I'm signing an order dismissing the case. Without prejudice. The government is free to refile the case provided they do so within the statute of limitations. Do you anticipate doing so, Mr. Latham?"

Siobhan watched Latham's face carefully and spied the defeat behind his grim expression. He wouldn't refile. Not this case. He'd go back to his office with the rest of his team and plot a bigger, badder case to try to crack the Mancuso family empire. He could plot all he wanted. She would be waiting, ready to block his every move.

An hour later, she stood on the sidewalk in front of the Earl Cabell Federal Courthouse with her driver slash bodyguard, Neal, and Jimmy standing beside her. "Stay clean, Jimmy.

They're not done with you. The best thing you can do for your don, for your family, is to keep a low profile."

"What am I supposed to do for work?"

She shook her head. She'd done her part and his livelihood wasn't her personal problem, but keeping him happy and working was part of a bigger business strategy and she recognized its importance. "Go home to your wife. Everything you need is there." She spoke slowly to emphasize the things she wouldn't say out loud. Odds were solid Don Carlo Mancuso's older daughter, Dominique, who ran the books for the family, had set Mrs. Girardo up with a big fat nest egg, guaranteed to keep Jimmy happy and silent as long as necessary. She would never know the details and she didn't want to, but it was hard to compartmentalize in the world she occupied, no matter how hard she tried. She turned to Neal. "Make sure he gets home. I have a stop to make." She held up her phone. "I'll call for a ride."

Neal stood at attention and narrowed her eyes. "I'll wait for you."

Neal was being protective. It was her job and Siobhan got it, but the constant presence of another person was sometimes suffocating, and she was agitated at the inability to go off on her own like a normal person. She kept her voice even to avoid appearing as if she was ungrateful. "I'm going shopping and I want to browse without an escort. Tell me you'd rather do anything but stand around while I look for a dress to wear to Celia's wedding," she added, knowing the idea of spending an afternoon in a dress shop would make Neal cringe.

"What about..." Neal didn't need to finish the sentence.

"I sent Dominique a text to let her know all is well, and I'll see Don Carlo at dinner. I'll be an hour tops. Come back and get me then."

Neal edged away, conflict flashing in her eyes, but ultimately, she decided—correctly—Siobhan's decision overrode any ideas she had about her duty. Neal pointed at the Rolex around her wrist—the one she'd given her as a bonus last year. "I'll be back in an hour and a half." She grinned. "I've seen you shop before. No way will you be finished in an hour."

She flashed her a smile and strode the short distance down the block. It was typical autumn in Dallas. The trees were bare, the grass looked dead, and everything was shadowy gray like an Ansel Adams photo with tall buildings taking the place of mountain vistas. The weather was its usual schizophrenic, cold enough for a coat if you were standing in the shade, but suffocating when the sun dipped out of the clouds. She shrugged out of her jacket and pushed through the door at Francine's custom dress shop, ready to slip into the midst of bored, rich housewives spending their husbands' money. She knew it sounded sexist, but a glance around and she was convinced her assessment was on point. The place was crowded with ladies who lunch.

Not that there was anything wrong with that, but she simply couldn't relate. She welcomed a break from the weight of her work, but being here was a temporary diversion. Later today, she'd be standing in front of Don Carlo, giving him the rundown on what had happened in court today and discussing plans for the next case the US Attorney had waiting for them. But right now, she was a regular person, shopping for an outfit to wear to a wedding.

"Ms. Collins?"

She looked up from the display to see Francine staring at her with an expectant expression. Damn. She'd hoped she could slip in and out without being detected, but Francine was a longtime friend of the family and would insist on making a fuss. "Good afternoon, Francine."

"Let me guess, you're looking for the perfect dress for the wedding next week."

Siobhan nodded, thinking the Mancuso family should hire Francine for her sleuthing skills. "Yes, and I'm afraid I've waited until the last minute, so it either needs to fit right off the rack or your tailor will need to work double-time."

Francine reached out a hand and squeezed her arm. "Not to worry. Don't I always take good care of you?"

Siobhan looked down at Francine's hand and resisted the urge to shrug out of her grasp. She knew others probably enjoyed Francine's maternal attention, but to her it was foreign, no matter how many times she encountered it. Still, she appreciated the service though she suspected it came partly from a desire to curry favor with her boss, whose daughters spent liberally at the flagship store. She forced a smile. "You do, and I don't know what I'd do without you." She glanced at her watch. "I have an hour."

A few minutes later, she was seated on a chaise, holding a glass of champagne, watching a parade of women modeling evening wear. The women were beautiful, and Siobhan wondered if the store kept a bevy of gorgeous models in the storeroom for wealthy customers or if Francine conjured them out of thin air. Didn't matter either way, but Siobhan did enjoy the show and the proximity of these women when her personal life didn't allow much time or discretion to indulge.

The first few dresses were unremarkable. She didn't want to stand out at the party and upstage Celia Mancuso, but she did want to feel confident in whatever she wore. Every detail of her appearance needed to bolster the authority that came with her role. The wedding of the younger daughter of the Mancuso family would be the event of the season, and everyone important to the family would be there, and many business deals would be initiated in side rooms during the event. Deals she would oversee.

She sipped the crisp, dry champagne, noting with appreciation Francine had brought out the expensive stuff. Too bad since she wouldn't finish the glass. It might be Friday afternoon happy hour for everyone else in the world, but she still had to report in to Carlo, and he respected a level head. She could relax later that evening, when she was back at her apartment—the only place she dropped her guard. She stared at the back of the model who was exiting the room and contemplated relaxation of a different kind when Francine's voice cut through her thoughts.

"I think this one is perfect."

Siobhan tore her gaze from the model and focused her attention to the front of the room. The midnight blue dress was beautiful, but the woman wearing it was truly stunning, her ocean blue eyes meeting hers as if to say, "Do you like what you see?"

She did. She liked it very much. "Yes, perfect." She turned to Francine. "May I have a moment? To determine if it suits me."

"Of course, dear." Francine motioned to her assistant to follow her as she exited the dressing area and closed the door behind them. The model stayed in place in the front of the room, silent and beautiful, but her eyes invited Siobhan to approach. She didn't wait to comply.

She touched the sleeve of the dress. "This fits you impeccably."

"It'll look even better on you," the model said.

"Do they pay you extra to flatter the customers?"

A smile. "It's all part of the package."

Siobhan kept her breath steady, which was a chore since her heart was racing. No wonder. She'd won in court and deserved a moment of celebration. Downing champagne this early in the day might be ill-advised, but giving in to the pull of attraction with a stranger might be exactly what she needed to cool her adrenaline. She reached up and ran a finger along the neckline of the dress, letting her touch linger on the silky skin at the hollow of the model's neck. "I'll have to try it on to see for myself."

The woman reached up a hand and placed it over Siobhan's. "Let me help you with that."

Siobhan watched as she deftly unzipped the back and stepped out of the dress, catching it with one hand before it slipped to the floor. She held it out like an offering, and Siobhan snatched it only long enough to toss it onto the chaise before turning back to the near-naked model standing before her. She was tall, tan, and flawless. Siobhan paused for a second, acutely conscious that the model might not feel like she had a choice here and, while she specialized in limiting choices when it came to business, this was pleasure, and the rules were different. "I'm no longer interested in the dress."

"But you have other interests."

"I do."

The model stepped forward and slid her hand under Siobhan's jacket. "So do I."

Siobhan sucked in a breath. She'd gone weeks, maybe months, without indulging her desires. "If you want to leave now, you should. I'll let Francine know you were very accommodating."

"I want you to undress. I want to help you with your fitting." She leaned in and whispered in Siobhan's ear. "I think you want what I'm offering. Am I right?"

"Yes." Once the word was out, giving in to her desire was easy and effortless. She shrugged out of her jacket and tossed it onto the chaise with the dress, no longer caring about the color, the fit, or anything else related to Celia's wedding. Girls like Celia could allow themselves to be sucked into the silliness of romance and glamour, but not her. Passion was something to be indulged and enjoyed, but she would never let it distract her from what was really important.

CHAPTER THREE

Royal stepped into her apartment and tossed her bag on the floor. She rubbed her shoulder, which was still sore from the car accident that fortuitously saved her life. Hell, her entire body was still sore, and all she wanted to do was crawl into bed and stay there until further notice.

First up, she needed some water—the pills they'd given her when she checked out of the hospital in El Paso left her parched. She walked to the kitchen, retrieved a glass from the cabinet, and held it under the faucet. While she waited for the glass to fill, she reached over and opened the door to the fridge, hoping she hadn't left anything odorous behind since she hadn't been here in over six months. To her surprise, a row of bottled water, a six-pack of beer, and a half gallon of milk greeted her. She pulled the top off the milk and held it a safe distance from her nose, but when no sour smell greeted her, she went on high alert. She quietly placed the jug back on the shelf, turned off the faucet, and drew her gun. She walked carefully back through the apartment, paying close attention to the signs she'd missed when she'd entered moments ago. Surfaces were free of dust, the air was fresh, and was that a plant on the dining room table? In all the years she'd used this place as her home base, she'd never had a plant, let alone one that looked freshly watered, and her brain struggled to process the idea of a burglar leaving a leafy gift behind.

A thump drew her attention to the hallway that led to the bedroom, signaling the burglar hadn't left yet. She moved quickly, but quietly, down the hall and pressed tightly against the wall outside of her bedroom. Another thump, followed by the sound of running water, and then footsteps headed in her direction. The burglar sure was making themselves at home. Not for long.

Gun first, she swung into the room and shouted, "Hands in the air!"

"What the hell, Royal!"

"Ryan?" She lowered her gun and shook her head at the sight of her younger brother standing in the center of her bedroom dressed in boxers and a T-shirt. "I thought you were a burglar."

He grinned. "Well, I did break in, but that was a month ago. I had a key made after that, so it was just the one time."

She pointed at the open closet, which was full of his clothes. "Looks like you've made yourself pretty comfortable."

"Well, I figured you could use someone to keep an eye on your place. You know, since you're never here. That's what I told the landlord, anyway."

Royal vowed to have words with Mr. Withers the next time she saw him. The old guy would call the cops if he heard any of the tenants making noise past midnight, but he didn't give a shit about handing out keys to anyone who asked. "And you figured you were that person?"

"Better me than some stranger."

He had a point. "True." She pointed at the empty Army-issue duffel bag in the corner. "Are you here for a while or do you have to ship out soon?" She watched his expression go blank and he looked away, avoiding her scrutiny. "What's up?"

"Are you hungry?" he asked, obviously trying to change the subject. "I can whip up some pancakes."

Her stomach rumbled at the mention of food and her memory of Ryan's pancakes. Hospital food had sucked, and the slice of greasy pizza the guys at the FBI field office in El Paso had served her during her debrief sent her system into revolt. All she'd been able to think about for the past few days was getting home, such as it was, and sacking out for the next few weeks, but now Ryan was here and it was clear he was holding on to something they needed to discuss. "Yeah, pancakes sound good. I'll take a shower while you cook."

She locked the door to the bathroom, craving uninterrupted privacy. It had been so long since she'd had the luxury of isolation, and she wanted to savor every moment. She turned the shower faucet handle to the hottest setting and stripped off her clothes, leaning into the mirror to inspect her bruises.

She'd woken up in the hospital in El Paso several days ago with a fellow FBI agent sitting guard beside her bed. He'd called the doctor, who informed her she was extremely lucky—she'd suffered a concussion, bruised ribs, and some scrapes, but she was otherwise okay. The ruckus she'd caused in the van had distracted Danny, causing him to run a red light at a high rate of speed, flipping the vehicle when he crashed into a bus crossing the intersection. The rear doors of the van had broken open and she'd shot out onto the side of the road. Danny had died in the accident, and Eduardo didn't fare much better. She was unconscious when she arrived at the hospital, but the ER nurse had called the emergency contact on her phone, which was the number for her handler, who'd made arrangements for the local field office to protect her until she was ready to be released.

That was what had really happened, but the official story was she'd died in surgery after the accident. It was a great cover, but she had regrets about not being able to witness the bureau take down the Garza family firsthand. This was better, though. They wouldn't come looking for her and she could finally be done working undercover. She knew plenty of colleagues who did this gig until they no longer remembered who they really were and they became unrecognizable to friends and family. She was teetering on the verge, and it was way past time to stop pretending to be someone she wasn't—no matter how much she excelled at it.

The shower was hot and she savored the comfort of the steam rising up from the tub and the pounding water against her neck. When she finally felt the muscles loosen, she let her mind wander to Ryan and what he was doing here, dressed in boxers in the middle of the day, with seemingly no place else to go. *He'll tell you when he's ready. Or you'll get it out of him one way or another.*

When the hot water had run completely out, she turned off the shower, toweled dry, and fished a pair of Army sweats out of her dresser drawer, noting Ryan's clothes lined up in neat piles next to hers. He really had moved in. She finger-combed her wet hair and then padded barefoot to the kitchen, where he was adding pancakes to an already perilously large stack.

He pointed at her with the spatula. "Do me a favor and butter these while they're still hot."

She reached for the butter and a knife, grateful for the menial and so very normal task. The pats of butter melted the second they touched the fluffy pancakes, and her stomach rumbled again. "These smell amazing."

"They should. I added extra vanilla to the batter."

"You learn that in the Army?"

"No, I didn't learn anything that useful in the Army."

She made a mental note of the growl in his voice and his use of the past tense, but she kept her tone neutral. "You want to talk about it?"

"No, but I guess I owe you an explanation."

He did and she wanted to hear it, but she also wanted to chill, and she suspected whatever he wanted to discuss would be the antithesis to relaxation. "Let's eat first and then we can talk."

"Fair enough. There's bacon in the oven. Grab that and I'll finish with these."

A few minutes later, they were perched on barstools at the kitchen pass-through, wolfing down pancakes and bacon. Royal ate way past when she was full, but the home-cooked food was impossible to resist after she'd been subsisting on takeout for months. Her entire plan for the day consisted of stuffing her face and then falling into bed and sleeping until she woke up from natural causes even if that wasn't for a few days. When she finally shoved her plate aside, Ryan spoke.

"I guess now is as good a time as any to talk."

Royal's phone buzzed. She shot a look at the screen, planning to turn off the ringer, but it was a text that read *Call me 911* from Mark Wharton, special agent in charge of the Dallas field office. "Crap. Hang on. I have to take this." She answered the call and walked into the bedroom, shutting the door behind her. "What's up?"

"Your debrief is scheduled for this afternoon."

"I already debriefed in El Paso."

"With the field office, yes, but the AUSA is here for a conference and he wants to talk to you."

"Are there cutbacks since I was last in the office?" she asked. "I don't recall you setting up appointments for me in the past."

"You're hilarious. I'm calling you because I'll be at the courthouse this afternoon, and I want you to come see me when you're done."

Something about his tone caused the hair to raise on the back on her neck. "I was planning to take some time off. I've got it coming. I'll do the debrief, but then I'm headed to the beach for a few weeks." The makeshift plan fell from her lips. Yes, she had been thinking about a vacation, a real one, for a while, but it was a distant imagining she hadn't assigned any specific detail to yet. Now that she'd voiced her preference for a locale, she warmed up to the idea. "I plan to sit on the sand with a bucket of beer and a good book." She gave it a beat, but he didn't respond before prodding. "I deserve it, don't I?"

He cleared his throat. "You deserve a lot, and you'll have it all someday. But right now, you're the best UC we have, and I have a case that can't wait."

"Wait, you want me to go undercover again?" Silence beat through the line, and her stomach roiled. "I told you, this was the last time."

"Come in and talk. That's all I'm asking."

It wasn't all he was asking. She knew it and he knew she knew it. He had the power to fire her if she said no, and she carefully weighed her options. This job was her life. She might not want to play pretend all the time, but her role as law enforcement and the relationships she'd made during her tenure defined her in a way that was all-consuming. If she quit, who would she be?

"I'll talk, you listen," he said, his voice pleading now.

"Come by after your appointment and hear what I have to say. Okay?"

She had a choice, but since making it might blow up her world, she opted to buy some time and hear him out. No harm could come from simply listening to what he wanted to say. "I promise to listen, but I'm making no other promises. Got it?"

"Got it. See you then."

Royal stared at the phone in her hand, but he was no longer on the line. What had she just gotten herself into? Could he seriously expect her to jump back into a case when she was only hours out of being someone entirely different? This couldn't be happening. Or could it?

"Royal, are you coming back out here?"

Ryan For a moment, she'd completely forgotten he was here, in her apartment, with stacks of pancakes at the ready. She might not have control over her own destiny, but she could find out what was going on with him. "On my way." She shoved her phone into her pocket and headed back to the kitchen. Ryan was seated at the table, a grim expression on his face. "You look sad," he said. "Do pancakes make you sad?"

She sighed. "I have to go to work."

"You just got back."

The undercurrent of pleading in his voice surprised her. "You know how it works." She pointed at the duffel bag in the corner again. "Duty calls, right?"

He didn't meet her eyes. "Yeah, right."

"You want to talk about it?"

"There's nothing to talk about."

"You've been here for a month and I get the feeling you're not in any hurry to get back, but you haven't found your own place, which tells me you're not out for good. Something's going on." She waited, and he finally met her gaze.

"I'm out. I don't have a job lined up, and I don't have a place to stay. It was between your apartment and the trailer park, and I knew you were gone, so I picked here. I can be out by the end of the day."

The despair in his voice was palpable, and as much as she wanted details, she knew he needed acceptance more. She reached across the table and grasped his hand. "Stay. As long as you want. I've got to be somewhere, but let's go get dinner tonight. Steaks. On me. We'll talk then. Okay?"

"Yeah, okay."

She resisted the urge to ask more and went into the bedroom to change. She ran through the selections in her closet and found a charcoal gray suit and a white shirt, still in the dry cleaning bag from when she'd picked them up from the cleaners months ago. As suits went, it was her favorite, but she'd much rather be wearing the sweats she had on. Every job demanded a costume of some kind, and today was headquarters at the FBI day, so she'd dress accordingly, but if things went her way, she'd never dress up as someone she wasn't again.

❖

Exactly an hour and a half after she'd entered, Siobhan strode out of Francine's shop, feeling ten times more relaxed than she had when she'd walked in. Celia's wedding was turning out to have hidden bonuses.

She reached into her purse to check her phone, acutely conscious of the fact she'd been off grid longer than usual. The first text was from Dominique. *Meeting before dinner. Don't be late.*

She checked the time, pleased to note that even with her excursion into Francine's she still had plenty of time to go home and change before heading to the Mancuso mansion. Dominique's text was completely unnecessary since she had never been late to anything. It wasn't her style. She typed a quick *I'll be there*, stepped off the curb, and started a new text to let her assistant know she would not be returning to the office. She barely typed three words before a loud shout and the roar of an engine revving jerked her attention from her phone, and she gasped at the sight of the SUV barreling straight toward her.

"Stop!"

She whipped her head around and saw a woman in a suit gesticulating wildly in her direction. She took a step back, but her heel caught on a grate. The woman stopped waving her arms and started running as the SUV bore down. Siobhan heard the screeching of tires and a second later, had the breath knocked out of her as hands grabbed her from behind and slammed her to the ground.

She lay quietly for a moment, in the arms of a stranger, struggling to process what had just happened.

"Are you okay?"

She turned to face her savior, surprised to see the person who'd rescued her was a woman. Her face was drawn in concern, her blue eyes both piercing and kind. "I think so." She shifted so she could sit upright. "What happened?"

The stranger reached over and brushed off her shoulders. "Not sure. Either that SUV had a very bad driver or he was trying to run you over." She pointed down the street. "Either way, he's gone."

Loud footfalls sounded on the pavement, and Siobhan saw Neal running toward her. She made a subtle motion with her hand, signaling for her to slow her approach. She turned back to the stranger, who had risen to a crouching position and was holding out a hand. She slipped her hand into the woman's, momentarily distracted by her warm hands and strong grip. She started to say something when she caught the woman grinning at her, and she couldn't help but grin back while she struggled to her feet, trying to balance on one heel.

"I think it's a goner." The woman pointed at the grate where her shoe was still wedged in the bars and bent at an angle that confirmed her analysis.

"I know I should be grateful just to be alive," Siobhan said, "but that's a vintage Louboutin, circa 1999."

"I have no idea what you just said." She pulled out her phone. "But we should call nine-one-one so you can file a report."

Siobhan shook her head. "I'd just feel stupid. Other than a broken shoe and feeling silly for not paying attention, there's been no harm."

The woman examined her closely before slipping her phone back into her pocket. She looked at Neal, who stood nearby. "She a friend of yours?"

"Yes."

"Then if you're okay, I need to go."

Siobhan wanted to offer her a reward, anything to get her to stay for a moment, so captivating were those eyes. "How can I thank you?"

The woman grinned again. "Maybe don't cross the street while texting in the future?" She touched a hand to her forehead as if in a tiny salute and walked away. Siobhan watched her go until Neal interrupted her thoughts.

"Are you okay?"

"Yes." She pointed at her shoe. "This is the only real casualty."

"Who was that?"

"A Good Samaritan. Did you get any info on the SUV?"

"Yes. We'll have Roscoe run the plate. It was coming straight for you. Someone is trying to send a message."

"Then we'll need to send one back. Let's go." Siobhan looked around for the woman who'd saved her, but she had disappeared from sight.

"You want me to go look for her?" Neal asked, following the line of her gaze.

She did, but her desire to see the woman again wasn't entirely rational and she needed to focus. "No. We should get going."

A few minutes later, as Neal navigated her way out of downtown, Siobhan couldn't help but scan the streets on the off chance she'd spot the woman, but no such luck. Probably for the best.

Traffic was unusually light, and they managed to swing by her place and still be at the gate to the Mancusos' on time. Lou, the guard, barely glanced into the car before waving them through. True, he knew her and Neal well, but she made a mental note to have a word with Michael, the head of security, about running some tests to make sure their first line of defense was never compromised.

Salvador, the Mancusos' houseman, was waiting for her at the front door after Neal dropped her off. "He's finishing up a call, but he asked me to have you go on in. Martini?"

An ice-cold martini sounded delicious, but the scene at the dress shop was as much as she was willing to let loose until after her meeting with Don Carlo. "That sounds perfect, but after. Okay?"

Sal nodded, his smile knowing and kind. He'd run the Mancuso household as long as she could remember, and he'd taken special care of her after her mother had died, making sure the kitchen always stocked her favorite macaroni and cheese, checking her homework, and telling her vague but comforting stories of her mother. She'd come a long way since the days she'd wandered through the house, a brooding child, and aside from Carlo, Sal had been the biggest constant in her life.

"Go ahead and have a drink, Shiv," Dominique called out as she swooshed into the room. "You don't have to be a suck-up all the time."

"Really?" Siobhan said, feigning disbelief. "I had no idea. I thought my sucking up was a requirement of being part of the family."

Dominique fixed her with a stare and then burst into laughter and Siobhan joined in. She was used to D's constant needling. When they were younger, it felt like the kind of teasing sisters did, but lately D's jabs were more frequent and less friendly. Even so, she'd long since stopped letting it get to her even if there might be an undercurrent of truth buoying Dominique's brash remarks. As for the drink, she'd stick with her plan to save it for later. Dominique, a Mancuso by blood, could drink all she wanted before meeting with her father because she didn't have anything to prove when it came to her role in the family, which made it difficult for her to understand Siobhan's delicate position. "Are you joining us?"

"I am and I hear alcohol is in order," Dominique said. "Sal, make my martini extra, extra dirty."

Sal nodded and raised his eyebrows at Siobhan as if to say are you sure you don't want one too, but she shook her head. Whatever Carlo wanted to discuss, she needed to keep a clear head.

She knocked on the door to the den, but before anyone responded, Dominique pushed her way in. Don Carlo Mancuso was seated behind his large desk, completely alone in the room, which was odd considering one of his capos was almost always in attendance. He smiled at the sight of his older daughter and waved them both into the room, rising to meet them.

Dominique reached for his hand and kissed it. "It's Friday, Poppa. Dinner is almost ready, and Celia and Tony will be here to discuss last-minute details about the wedding. Maybe take a break for a few hours?"

He waved her off. "I will, but we have a few things to discuss that won't keep." He motioned to Siobhan, who'd hung back to let Dominique have a moment with her father before they got down to business. "Come closer. I want to see that you are unharmed."

Siobhan ignored Dominique's questioning look and stepped closer to Carlo, who embraced her with a rare show of affection "*Patatino,*" he said, using the endearment she remembered from her youth. "You must be more careful."

"I will. Michael is looking into it."

"Siobhan will outlive us all, Poppa," Dominique said. This time her voice held more edge than tease.

"She may," Carlo said. "She is made of strong stuff." He patted Siobhan's arm. "Bring Michael's report to me personally. This deed will not go unpunished."

Out of the corner of her eye, Siobhan saw Dominique tilt her glass and down the rest of her martini. Time to change the subject before the mood in the room shifted into a darker space. "Court went well today. The judge sided with us. Jimmy's case was dismissed." She paused for a moment, knowing she had to tell the whole story or risk it coming back to bite her later. "For now. This prosecutor will keep coming, and I expect if there is any way he can bolster the evidence he has, he'll refile the case. Jimmy understands he's to lay low for now. He's not happy about not working, but I was clear it's not an option."

"He'll try to work," Carlo said, shaking his head.

"I explained to him that is not an option. Under any circumstances," Siobhan said.

"He doesn't need to work. His family will be fine," Dominique said. "Believe me, I arranged for the delivery myself."

Carlo frowned at Dominique's tone. "His wife and children are innocent, and we have an obligation to make sure they are taken care of. I would do the same for any one of you."

Siobhan was certain she understood the meaning, even if he wouldn't say the exact words in front of her. If Jimmy tried to work, to expose the family in any way, his family might be fine, but he would be out of the picture. She understood the consequence as well as if he'd outlined it for her, but without hearing the exact words, she was insulated from whatever might happen if Jimmy broke the family rules. She'd been as insulated as possible from the start. "Of course, Don."

"Sit, both of you," he said. "There's something else we need to discuss."

Siobhan shot a look at the closed office door, wondering again why she and Dominique were the only ones present for this meeting and assuming the worst. Carlo's next words confirmed her suspicions.

"I wish I could say I was surprised by what happened to our precious Siobhan today, but I'm not. This is only the beginning. I'm getting reports from our capos. Several of our businesses have suffered significant losses lately—theft of merchandise, vandalism, poor reviews. Someone is working to betray the family."

CHAPTER FOUR

Royal walked out of her debrief session and wandered through the US Attorney's office looking for her boss, half hoping he'd have already bugged out for the weekend. No such luck. SAC Mark Wharton was waiting for her in a conference room, and he stood to greet her when she walked in.

"Have a seat," he said, motioning to a chair across the table from where he'd been seated.

She hesitated. "I was hoping this would be a quick, stand and talk kind of conversation."

"It's not."

Resigned, but not defeated, she sat in the chair across from his desk but didn't settle in. "Debrief went fine."

"You did great work."

"Is that why I'm no longer on the case?"

"It's easier this way. Sending you back in would've raised too many questions. We have plenty on the Garzas at this point. Like I said, you did good work."

"Fine. Then you won't mind if I take a nice long vacation."

He narrowed his eyes. "That's new."

He wasn't wrong. She'd banked weeks of well-earned

days off, and she couldn't remember ever taking more than one day off at a time, and even then, it was usually to take care of an errand, not for recreation. "Is that a problem?"

"It's not, but the timing may be off. We have an emergent situation."

There it was. She tensed at the dread of what he was about to ask. "I'm not your only agent."

"True, but you're my best. You have only yourself to blame. I need someone who can jump in without a lot of prep time."

"And if I say no?"

"I'm not actually asking, but don't make me say that."

"I could quit."

"Sure, you could. Give up your retirement. Is that what you really want?"

It was a fair question, but she wasn't sure she had a ready answer. She'd thought about quitting before, but the idea had never been serious, and she'd sure never said it out loud. Speaking the words now sparked a relieved burst of freedom. She could get another job. Something in security. She knew agents who'd tripled their salary in the private sector, and she was better than every single one of them. And that was the crux of it. Without the job, she didn't have an identity because the job had been all about assuming someone else's. Maybe this was all she was good at, but the only way to find out was to walk away, and she wasn't ready to take that step. "What's the job?"

"You've seen the Mancuso family mentioned in the daily briefs?"

Royal nodded. "I'm familiar with their operation, generally speaking."

"We have a CI who's made inroads with the family, but he's gone about as far as he could go in the organization."

"And you think I'd get further? Key word 'he.' Mancuso is not going to let a woman hang out with made men."

"I guess you didn't drill deep on the briefs. Mancuso's only children are daughters, and the older one helps to run the family business." Wharton reached into a folder on his desk and pulled out a photo and handed it her way. "That's her. Dominique."

Royal stared at the photo. Dominique was beautiful, and her sexy smile likely garnered lots of attention. "So, she's in charge of his operations?" she asked.

"Kind of. Our intel says she runs the books. But his real right hand is his consigliere, Siobhan Collins. She may as well be one of his children since he practically raised her. If you haven't been up against her in court, you've missed a bruising."

"She's a real lawyer, not just a counselor to the don?"

"Yes, and she's ruthless, but our inside sources say she has a weakness."

"Really, what's that?"

"Tall, dark, and female. It's her type and you fit the bill."

Royal shook her head. "Nope. Get someone else."

"You're the best I've got."

He was right. She was the best at her job because it was easier to pretend to be someone she wasn't than face her own reality, but what he was asking now was different. He was asking her to take this job because of who she was, not who she could pretend to be, and the idea of it made her feel uncomfortably vulnerable. She started to say no, but he opened his desk drawer, pulled a photo out, and tossed it onto the desk. Her gut clenched and she reached for it.

"What?" he asked.

"This is her? Siobhan?"

"Yes. I thought seeing her might cause you to change your mind."

Royal stared at the photo, as captivated by Siobhan on paper as she had been when she'd seen her earlier that afternoon. She noted that unlike Dominique, Siobhan hadn't smiled for the photo. Instead, she wore an enigmatic expression, and Royal had a deep desire to know what she was thinking. She set the photo back on his desk and stabbed at it with her finger. "I have seen her. About thirty minutes ago. Someone tried to run her down in front of that store next to Neiman's, down the street." She told him about her encounter with Siobhan.

"You're fucking kidding me," he said. "What did you say to her? Does she know you're a cop?"

Royal shook her head. "I didn't say a word, and her bodyguard, some woman who looked like a WNBA center, showed up right away."

Wharton pulled another photo from the file. "Was this the bodyguard?"

"Yep. She looks way taller in person."

"She should. Name's Neal Walsh. Not WNBA, but she did play college ball. It's a mystery how she wound up on the Mancuso payroll. Did they see you come in here?"

Royal replayed the scene with Siobhan in slow motion. The gunning of the SUV's engine, the squeal of tires, her own voice shouting for Siobhan to get out of the street accompanied by the rapid pounding of her heart when she realized Siobhan was stuck on the grate and unable to get out of the way. Footfalls pounding the pavement—her own, followed by the thud as she crushed Siobhan against her and threw them both to the ground. After their initial exchange, Royal had slipped away, taking a shortcut through the Adolphus Hotel. At the time, she hadn't been concerned about being watched, only about getting to the office so that she could get this meeting over with. "No. Neal hustled her out of there pretty quickly."

He stared at the photos, his head slowly bobbing up

and down in a gesture Royal recognized as deep thinking mode. "Maybe we can work this to our advantage," he said. "Siobhan's going to trust the person who saved her life, right?"

"I hope you have a better cover than that planned. If she's the consigliere to Mancuso, she's going to make sure anyone who gets close to him is legit." For the first time since they'd started talking, Royal started to warm up to the idea of this op. She proceeded cautiously. "What is the cover?"

"Bar services and liquor vendor. They run their bootlegging and money laundering through their catering business, so the best way to get a firsthand look at the action is to be part of their supply chain. There are a bunch of businesses in town that feed into their catering business—florists, equipment rentals, liquor distributors and wholesalers—that they actually own on the sly. I figure you know everything you need to about alcohol and we've got an agent working TABC who'll vouch for you as someone who's connected and knows how to work the liquor laws. The manager for one of Mancuso's main liquor vendors, Valentino's, also provides bar services for parties, and they just got busted by TABC. One of their conditions for keeping their license is that they fire the guy, which causes them a problem since their biggest event of the year is scheduled for next week."

"What's this big event?"

"Mancuso's younger daughter, Celia, is getting married. The wedding will be the perfect opportunity for you to get a lot of solid intel on Mancuso's inner circle. The reception is at his estate, and everyone who's connected to him will be there and you'll have the run of the place. Saving Collins from getting run over in the street gives you even better odds of getting in under their radar."

"You don't know that she'll even be involved in the planning for the wedding. Plus, why would they trust a stranger to be part of the wedding? If all the families are going to be there, it's high risk for them to let anyone in who hasn't been properly vetted."

"True, but we've developed a solid cover. Our guy inside will introduce you as his cousin from Houston who's ready to step in and save the day."

"UC or CI?" she asked. If—big if—she took this gig, she preferred not to have to maneuver around another undercover officer.

"You'll be the only undercover on the case, but the UC on a related case will make the introductions. This op is very important."

"So important that you just now decided to add me to the team?"

He shrugged. "You know how it is. We've been close to nailing some of their people before, but this is the first time we've had a legit opportunity to get this close to the senior members of the family."

"And you think sending in a bartender will do the trick?" Posing as a bartender was how she'd managed to make contacts within the Garza cartel.

"Not a bartender, a 'manager.'" He used air quotes as if that would make it sound better. "And you underestimate how important bar services are to their operation. They run all their money through the catering business, and in order to keep up a show of legitimacy, they have to have a supplier that makes a show of abiding by state regulations while still being willing to help them launder funds. The CI helped us bust the current manager, and I have a feeling the family will see he never works again after he exposed them to potential shutdown. The setup is perfect. We've laid the foundation. You just need to win them over."

"Just?" Royal mentally ticked through all the reasons this

was a bad idea. There was no such thing as a perfect setup, and she was used to having a lot more lead time on a gig like this with plenty of preparation and thorough vetting. Walking in blind increased the likelihood of mistakes. Mistakes that could get her killed—not the way she wanted to end her career as an undercover agent. She should take her brush with death on the Garza case as a sign she'd used up the luck that had followed her throughout her career and move on.

But then an image of Siobhan Collins flashed in her mind, arousing her curiosity, among other things. Despite the broken shoe that caused her to pitch headlong into the street, she seemed confident and self-assured, and she was definitely gorgeous. How had she become the voice that whispered in the ear of the head of the most powerful crime family in Dallas? Was there an as yet unexposed vulnerability there? One she could exploit to expose the Mancuso family to prosecution?

The only way to find out was to accept this assignment. Was it worth it? Probably not, but when she opened her mouth, her response fell short of refusal. "If I do this, I have terms."

"Name them, but do it fast. We've got a cover ready for you and the opportunity to infiltrate starts next week. You'll need to spend time between now and then getting briefed on how their operation works. It's not a lot of time, but I know you can do it."

Royal ticked off her conditions. "I run the op. I don't need a handler. You can assign someone to be my contact, but I'm in charge." She pointed at her chest. "I'll take advice, but not orders."

"Look, Royal, I trust you completely, but this is too big a job for anyone to handle on their own."

She stood. "Then get anyone else to do it. I'm going on vacation."

She was a step away from the door when he called out, "Wait."

"Yes?" she asked without turning around.

"Your op, your way."

Words she'd waited to hear, but now that she had, was it enough to entice her to take on one last personality other than her own?

❖

Monday night, Siobhan walked past Neal and her lieutenant, Pete, and entered her penthouse apartment. She resented their constant presence but knew Carlo was right to add the protection in view of the close call she'd had on Friday. She changed into her favorite set of jade silk pajamas, poured a glass of red Zinfandel, and placed an order from the Thai restaurant down the street. She'd had back-to-back hearings in federal court and figured she deserved the indulgence. While she waited for the food to arrive, she reviewed the papers their contact in the police department had sent over about the SUV that had tried to run her down.

The car was registered to a local moving business who'd reported it stolen Friday morning. Neither she nor Neal had gotten a look at the driver, but she was fairly certain that even if she had, it wouldn't be helpful since whoever had been sending the message had likely paid somebody else to do their dirty work. But why had she been the target? Was it simply by virtue of her position within the family or was the villain targeting her for a specific reason? She took a deep drink of the wine, savoring the peppery finish on her tongue. Whatever the reason for the attack, it had shaken her up more than she cared to admit. She was no stranger to the danger that came from being part of this family, but she had managed to stay several layers away from the reality of it. Dispensing advice, defending family interests in court—her law degree didn't entirely insulate her from the risks, but the don did his best to shield her from the consequences of the family's enterprises. A fact she'd underappreciated until Friday, because if that woman hadn't stepped in, she might be dead.

Multiple times today, Siobhan had cursed the fact she'd failed to get the woman's name. Never mind that she'd been a bit in shock after having been thrown to the ground. She should've gotten the info to be able to send a thank you. Or perhaps even deliver one in person. The woman was a little masculine of center compared to her usual type, but she was striking, and those eyes... Siobhan hadn't been able to stop thinking about losing herself in those indigo eyes, and for a moment she allowed herself to bask in the fantasy of walking into Celia's wedding with the tall, gorgeous stranger on her arm.

She shook away the thought. She didn't have time for those kind of indulgences. Not with enemies focused on the family. Security at the wedding needed to be tighter than usual, and though the family had plenty of people who could make that happen, if something went wrong, she would deem it a failure on her part. She opened her laptop and did a few quick searches to check out the company who owned the vehicle, but they didn't appear to have any connections to Mancuso enemies, which meant their report of it having been stolen was likely true. She might not ever find out the name of the driver who'd tried to run her down last week, but all she had to do was wait. Whoever was out for her would try again.

A knock shook her from staring at the computer, and she walked to the door and looked through the viewer to see Neal, holding up two bags of food. She opened the door and held out her hand.

"Smells good," Neal said as she held the bags out to her.

"I ordered enough for you and Pete," she said, handing one back.

"We're good, thanks."

"I thought you liked Thai."

She rubbed her stomach. "I do, but I had jalapeños on my burger at lunch. No sense adding on. Pete just ordered himself a pizza."

"You should go get some dinner."

She shook her head.

"Seriously, Neal. I'm in for the night. You've done your job. Besides, it spooks me to have you sitting out here."

"Marco will be here in an hour to take over. I'll leave then. Order came straight from the don that we aren't to leave you alone."

She wanted to say she was missing the point—that she didn't want anyone lurking outside her door—but it wasn't worth fighting a battle she couldn't win. She had a lot of pull in the organization, but Carlo had the final word.

The food was spicy and wonderful, and paired with the bold Zin, it almost distracted her enough to relax for a few minutes. She finished her food, leaned back on the couch, and closed her eyes, letting her mind roam. It settled on the model at Francine's, whose talent modeling dresses was only surpassed by her talent with her tongue, and then quickly faded into an image of the tall, dark stranger who'd pulled her from danger last week. Two very different women, each desirable in their own unique way. Focusing on these two encounters combined with the serotonin from the spicy food and wine had her growing aroused. With a glance to the door to make sure she'd thrown the security lock, she pushed aside the tie of her robe and slid her hand down the length of her abdomen and traced her fingers lightly over her thighs before dipping between her legs to begin a steady rhythm. Within moments, she was wet and her breath was labored. She closed her eyes again and amped up the arousal by imagining she was back in the stranger's arms. But this time she wasn't lying in the street in downtown Dallas, but here in her apartment where she could offer a proper thank you.

CHAPTER FIVE

I f you need me to leave, I will."
    Royal stood in the center of her apartment with a packed suitcase at her feet. Ryan was lounging on the couch where he'd spent most of the time since she'd been back. "Stay as long as you want," she replied. "I don't know how long I'll be gone."

"Let me guess, you can't tell me where you're going either. Right?"

She shrugged, torn between telling him she would only be across town and not saying anything at all. "You of all people should know how that goes. Care to share how many ops you've run?"

Instead of answering, he grunted and fiddled with the TV remote. She still didn't know why he'd left the Army. The brief window of time he'd been willing to talk on the day she returned home had closed when she'd been called to the US Attorney's office. She'd lobbed opportunities to reopen the discussion several times in the past week, but he wasn't biting other than to assure her it was an honorable discharge and that MPs wouldn't come looking for him. "If you want to talk about it, I'm here," she said in a final effort to get him to talk.

"Well, you're not actually since you've got one foot out the door."

He made like he was joking, but the laugh was fake, and it made him sound kind of whiny. It wasn't like him to feel sorry for himself, so Royal wondered what was going on. If she were a good sister, she'd probably stick around and wait him out until he was ready to spill about why he'd gone from Army Ranger to couch surfer all of a sudden. But she had to go and he didn't appear ready to open up to her anyway.

"What do I do if there's an emergency?" Ryan asked.

She started to tell him to call her, but she wasn't taking her personal phone. She had a new ID, a new phone, new everything, and the fewer people who knew about it, the better. She felt a little bit guilty about it, but not enough to compromise her cover. "I'll check in with you when I can. If something goes wrong with the apartment, call Mr. Withers. The bureau will contact you if something happens to me."

"You're definitely cut out for this line of work."

She heard the edge in his voice and almost didn't bite. "Go ahead, say what's on your mind."

"You get to wall yourself off from real connections, real feelings, while you play pretend. You don't have to get close to anyone because none of it is real."

"What the hell happened to you out there?" she asked, unable to keep back the question and certain him lashing out at her was some form of projection. "Whatever it was, I'm here for you if you want to talk about it, but don't take your anger out on me."

He sighed. "Sorry." He pointed at the door. "Go, do your thing. Be the hero. One of us should make something of their life."

She didn't want to leave things like this between them.

She didn't want to leave at all. But she'd made a promise and she was going to keep it. This would be the last time. It had to be.

Thirty minutes later, she pulled into the parking lot for Valentino's. The bleached blonde at the desk was chatting on the phone and waved her toward the two metal chairs in the tiny waiting area. Royal spent the wait scoping out the place, and so far, she wasn't impressed. Peeling paint on the walls, scuffed wood floors, and rickety furniture. Hopefully, Robert Valentino had a better setup to meet actual clients because with what she was seeing now, she wouldn't hire his company for a backyard barbecue, let alone an event of the year wedding.

"I know, right? That's what I said."

Royal looked up at the receptionist for a moment, but quickly realized she was still talking to whoever was on the other end of the phone line. Gossiping, no doubt. She made a mental note to be careful around her and also to snoop when she could. Office staff who didn't think anyone noticed them were prime sources of information.

She was still listening to the side of the call she could hear when the door to the inside burst open and a tall, thin, sandy-haired guy appeared. Royal recognized him as the owner from his photo in the bureau's file, but she feigned nonchalance.

"Royal?"

She stood and clasped his outstretched hand. "That's me."

"Robert Valentino. Come on back." He held open the door for her, but his eyes were on the receptionist and he drew his hand across his throat. "Enough with the personal calls, Sandy."

With a wistful glance toward the now huffing Sandy, Royal followed Robert into the inner sanctum, which was as ratty as the rest of the place. The walk to Robert's office was short, putting to rest any chance the hallway might lead to a more plush facility. At Robert's direction, she took a seat in one of the chairs identical to those in the waiting area.

"My cousin Dean vouches for you. Says you know your stuff."

"He's right." She'd only met Dean DeLuca the day before yesterday, an introduction arranged by another undercover agent working a related case. Dean ran a huge equipment rental operation, and the majority of his business was for the Mancusos. She'd wondered if Dean was the confidential informant, but she wouldn't know for sure while she was working this case since the bureau preferred to keep UC connections double-blind. She hadn't even met the UC who'd arranged the intro to Dean, but Dean had spoken highly of him, so his reference got her in the door, and she'd made enough of an impression on Dean for him to vouch for her with Robert. These guys were shrewd, but personal relationships were everything, and once you made a connection, you had an in. "He would know," she said, tossing in the compliment to gauge Robert's response.

"He would. Guy runs a tight ship." Robert nodded. "We've got a big job this weekend and I need someone who can manage all the logistics. You do good and there might be other opportunities that open up, if you know what I mean."

"Dean said you would take good care of me if I took good care of your business." She settled back in her chair, not wanting to appear too eager.

"Dean was right. You just have to earn your spot like the rest of us."

"Got it," she replied, wondering how many times he was going to emphasize the point. "What's the big job?"

"It's Celia Mancuso's wedding."

She gave a low whistle, knowing he would expect her to be suitably impressed. "I heard about it. That is a big job."

"You up for it?"

"I'm up for whatever you've got. Where are we doing this?"

"Word is she wanted to do the wedding at one of those rent-a-castle places, do some fairy tale decorating shit, but her dad put his foot down and the wedding is at the Mancuso estate. It's in Preston Hollow, but deep in the center, like you'd never see it from the road. Security is locked up tighter than the Bush house a few blocks away. Makes setup a little more difficult, but Don Carlo likes to host on his home turf, if you know what I mean. We do a lot of work for the family business and we'll go wherever."

"Got it. Makes sense. Do you do a lot of work for them personally or just for their business?" she asked, hoping the question wasn't too much too soon, but wanting to be clear.

"Like there's a difference. They don't throw a lot of family social events, but when they do, they come to us. Business-wise, we handle all of their bar needs. They're our number one client."

Royal chanced a glance around the room. *And probably your only ones.* Which explained the run-down office. Who needed to spruce things up when you already had a captive client to fund your business? "Tell me what you need me to do."

"You'll be my right hand. What I really need is someone to run point and make sure the bar setups are done, that all the bartenders check out—TABC-wise and for the family's security. There's going to be a lot of important people there. You'll need to handle anything that comes up. I'll be at the party, but as a guest, and I'd like to enjoy myself. Got it?"

Royal recognized his attempt to establish rank, quick and early. They weren't at the point where Robert was comfortable enough to reveal he was a newly made capo for Mancuso, but he wanted her to know he was important and deserved her respect. "Got it. You're in charge, but my ass is on the line if anything goes wrong." She smiled to show she didn't mind him lording it over her. If only.

He reached over and clapped her on the shoulder. "Exactly." He stood. "Come on, let's go check out the place."

She followed him again, thinking she was getting a tour of the building, but he led her out the back door to a Cadillac Seville. He tossed her the keys. "You drive. I like to ride."

A few turns later, she realized they were headed in the direction of Mancuso's place. She hated that she wasn't in her own ride, that she didn't know exactly where they were going, and didn't know what to expect when she got there, but she was experienced enough not to let her discomfort show. A few minutes later, they pulled up at a guard gate and Robert gave his name to the man on duty, who waved them through. The driveway was long and winding, but eventually, the enormous mansion came into view. For a minute, she thought she'd been transported to Tuscany—the place looked like an Italian villa with arched entries leading to several tiered buildings. Lush gardens lined the wide circular drive.

Robert motioned for her to park close to the house. "Nice place, huh?" he said as they got out of the car.

"Very," Royal said, certain there were some people in the world who liked living in opulent grandeur, but she wasn't one of them. Her apartment, where she knew where everything was and where she could see any trouble headed her way, suited her fine. But she could tell Robert was impressed, maybe even envious, of this palace, so she pretended a little harder. "It's enormous. How many people live here?"

"Don Carlo, of course. His wife died years ago. God rest her soul. The don has two daughters. The older one, Dominique, works directly with him and she keeps an apartment on the grounds, but she's got a place downtown too. Her little sister Celia's been living here, but that all changes after the wedding."

Royal had hoped he'd mention Siobhan Collins, but she wasn't going to bring her up on her own. As the don's trusted counselor, she'd definitely be at the wedding. The key was figuring out how to get close to her, and she had two tools to make that happen—patience and trusting her instincts.

The elderly uniformed man who answered the door nodded at Robert and took a moment to look Royal up and down to the point Royal wondered if he was a capo disguised as a butler. "We were expecting you and Leo," he said, directing his comment to Robert.

"Hey, Sal," Robert said. "This is Royal. Leo was filling in, but she's taking over."

Royal held out her hand to the man and said, with as much respect as she could summon, "Nice to meet you."

"Wait here."

Royal watched him turn sharply on his heel, a smooth, dancer-like move that belied his age. He was gone from the room in a flash. "What was that about? I thought you said I had this job?"

"Cool it," Robert said. "Everything's going to be fine. This is protocol. Maybe you haven't done a big important event like this before, but there's safety considerations and everyone needs to be vetted."

"So you vouching for me isn't enough?"

"It would be if he hadn't only just been made."

Royal resisted turning around at the sound of the familiar voice. She shouldn't recognize it since she'd only spent a moment in conversation with the woman who owned it, but she did and it sent a thrill down her spine like it had the first time she'd heard Siobhan speak. Royal raised an eyebrow at Robert, who was looking pretty flustered. "Is that true, Robert? And here I thought I was coming to work for a big player." Before he could respond, Royal turned to face Siobhan, who took a sharp breath when they locked eyes.

"If it isn't the life-saving stranger from downtown."

Royal tuned in to the tone behind the words, but she couldn't tell if Siobhan was praising or making fun of her. "Stranger? I hardly think we're strangers now." She spotted Robert looking back and forth between them, unable to fathom what they could be talking about, but she had no desire to explain to him. In fact, all she wanted was to have a moment alone with Siobhan.

"True," Siobhan said. "Robert, I'm going to borrow your friend for a moment." She started to walk away, pausing after a few steps to turn her head and ask, "Are you coming?"

Royal grinned. "Absolutely."

❖

Siobhan resisted looking back again, letting the sound of Royal's footfalls be the only signal she was still behind her as she led the way to the den she used as an office when she was at the Mancuso mansion. The long walk through the hallways of the house gave her time to digest the surprise of having the stranger who'd saved her life show up with Robert, but she was consumed with curiosity, and she wanted to ask her questions in private.

She took the formal route rather than the secret back ways she'd learned as a child when she'd learned to navigate her way from the kitchen, where her mother worked, to the landing where she played games with Dominique and Celia, and then back to the servants' quarters where she'd been raised until the family had taken her into the big house as one of their own.

"This is a beautiful home."

Royal's voice was smooth and husky, and Siobhan melted into the sultry tone. "I like that you called it a home. Most people who come here for the first time, use words like mansion and compound, house at the very least, but home always seems so simple and not worthy for them. but it's exactly how I think of this place."

"Do you live here?"

Royal's question seemed innocent on its face, but it alerted Siobhan she'd overshared. She pointed to a door up ahead on the right. "This is my office." She pushed through the door and pointed to a chair near her desk. "Have a seat."

She slid into the seat behind the desk, enjoying the boundary it provided, and crossed her hands. "I wanted to thank you properly for saving me, but when I finally caught my breath, you were gone. And now you show up here. How opportune." She left the words hanging in the air, wondering if Royal would offer an explanation for her appearance. It might be nothing more than a coincidence, but she hadn't gotten to where she was in life without looking beneath the surface of everyone's actions.

Royal crossed her legs and leaned back in the chair, confident and comfortable—two qualities Siobhan wasn't used to seeing on someone who'd been summoned to her office. "Definitely opportune. I had an appointment that day I couldn't miss, or I would've stuck around to make sure you were okay. Let's just say that spending time with you would've been preferable to the meeting with the IRS agent I had scheduled."

Siobhan purposely ignored the flirty undertone. "Tax troubles?"

"No trouble. I simply had to explain why I was right. I was successful."

"Are you often successful?"

"I like to think so."

"How long have you worked for Robert?"

"Believe it or not, we met for the first time today. Through a mutual friend, Dean Deluca. Maybe you know him?"

Royal's pause before answering was barely perceptible, but Siobhan was used to detecting nonverbal cues. "I do. How do you know him?"

"I helped a friend of his out with a delicate matter. I ran an operation in Houston similar to Valentino's, and when Robert's last manager ran into trouble, Dean recommended me as a good fit to fill in at the last minute. I understand this wedding will be the social event of the season."

Siobhan nodded. All anyone had been able to talk about lately was Celia's wedding, but she couldn't wait until it was over and she could turn her attention back to other family business that needed tending. "Robert has worked with us for a long time. If he and Dean vouch for you, then you must be good at what you do."

"I am." Royal flashed a cocky smile. "I'll show you."

Siobhan didn't return the smile. Yes, she wanted to flirt back, but not if Royal was going to be working with them. She didn't play where she worked. It was bad for business, and business always came first. "How about you show all of us at the wedding. Celia has been planning this day since she was a little girl, and we all want it to be extra special. When your predecessor was arrested, it was an unpleasant surprise, and we don't want any more of those. Okay?"

Royal nodded slowly. "Okay. No surprises." She drummed her fingers on the arm of her chair. "Was vetting me the only reason you asked to see me alone, then?"

Right, that. "Not the only reason. I wanted to thank you properly for rescuing me last week. Damn heel nearly killed me."

Royal grinned again. "It was a gorgeous shoe, and to be clear, it was the SUV that nearly killed you, not the shoes. Your security detail should be more careful with you."

Siobhan nearly confessed she'd ditched them for the rendezvous with the shop model, but she stopped before oversharing that little tidbit. What was it about this woman that made her lose her composure? All she could think about right now was the way she'd felt tucked in Royal's arms, lying in the street. Not her best moment, but not the worst either. "How about you focus on your job and I'll worry about my own safety from here on out?"

Royal raised her palms. "Sure. Whatever you like."

Siobhan waited, but apparently that was all Royal had to say. This woman's presence was disconcerting. Time to end this meeting before she grew more distracted, but she still hadn't done what she'd brought Royal here to do. She reached into her desk and pulled out a business card, the fancy ivory linen stationery feeling good against her fingers. She uncapped her favorite Visconti pen and scrawled her cell phone number on the back of the card before handing it across the desk. Royal reached for her outstretched hand, and for a second their fingers touched with a buzz of electricity.

"What's this?"

"My personal number."

"In case I want to ask you out on a date?"

Siobhan choked a laugh. "I don't date. But I do return favors and I owe you. Save that for when you need something truly important."

Royal examined both sides of the card and blew on the still drying ink from Siobhan's pen. As Siobhan watched her tuck the card in her jacket, she felt heat rise from her neck to her face and prayed she wasn't turning red. This was getting ridiculous—acting like a schoolgirl with her first crush. She stood. "Robert's probably wondering if we've tossed you into the secret dungeon."

"There's a secret dungeon? I'm intrigued."

"Of course you are." Siobhan rolled her eyes and then led the way back downstairs, where they found Robert flirting with one of the maids. Typical. Made guys always acted like any female in their vicinity was hot for them. She glanced at Royal and wondered why she didn't find her flirting offensive in the same way. It was different. Like they were both on the same level, unlike the maid who had no choice but to put up with the macho act or risk losing her job. Royal frowned at Robert—only for a second, but long enough to signal she didn't approve of his macho routine. Maybe it was because Royal was a woman, or maybe she was simply a different breed than the guys who usually came around. Siobhan wished she didn't care which, but she felt invested in this woman who'd stepped out of her normal routine to step in front of a moving vehicle to save her life.

"She check out okay?" Robert asked.

"Feel free to show her around the property," Siobhan said, ignoring the more direct question. "The don is in a meeting. Make sure you do not disturb him." She hesitated a second before walking away. Long enough to catch Royal's eye and share a nod. There was definitely a connection there. What was she going to do about it?

CHAPTER SIX

Royal pulled the suit bag from her closet and unzipped the zipper. If she'd known she'd have to wear a tux for this gig, she would've told her boss to shove it. He must've known because it was lurking in the closet when she'd moved in along with a bunch of other stuff. Books, knickknacks. A casual observer wouldn't be able to tell she'd moved in just last week, and that was the whole idea.

She dried her hair and stared at her reflection in the mirror. She didn't see it, but plenty of women had told her she was good-looking, and she'd never had any trouble capitalizing on her appearance, especially when it came to her job. She could definitely tell Siobhan had been intrigued but hadn't fallen all over herself the way some women did, and Royal respected her for being impervious to her playful flirtation. Siobhan was a serious woman, and it would take a serious amount of effort to get close to her.

She'd read the dossier on Siobhan, and while it was illuminating, it left more questions than answers. Siobhan had spent her youth at the Mancuso mansion. Her mother had been an employee on the household staff, and Siobhan had grown up with the Mancuso children, forming a close bond with the family. Her mother died when she was ten, but instead of being shuttled off to live with some other relatives, Siobhan stayed at the mansion, where Carlo Mancuso took a personal interest in her education. She attended Tulane Law School, returning after graduation to open a private practice that, as far as anyone could tell, was devoted to one client only—the Mancuso family. She was regularly in court with OC goons, but the rumor was her real expertise was advising the don about his business interests and she was actually his chief consigliere.

It was highly unusual for an old school crime family to have a female consigliere, let alone one as young as Siobhan, but Mancuso was known for bucking trends. Although his younger daughter, Celia, was more of an appear on the society page type, Dominique reportedly had a large role in the crime family's operations.

Royal slipped into the tux and tied the damn bow tie, cursing her boss for not providing the clip-on kind. She flashed to an old memory of tying a bow around Ryan's neck when he was getting ready for prom and she wondered how he was doing. Something big was going on with him, but she knew no amount of pressuring him was going to make him share. She got it. She'd been in the military too and had witnessed things she'd give anything not to have seen. Was he still at her apartment? It was a forty-five-minute drive away if she wanted to check, but she didn't plan to risk a visit while she was undercover. Too easy to slip up and get made. She'd find a way to contact him once she was fully settled in.

A knock on the door shook her out of her thoughts. She wasn't expecting anyone, and she considered ignoring the interruption, but a few seconds later, the knocking grew louder in what sounded like someone pounding their fists against the door. Whoever it was, wasn't giving up, and she strode to the front of the house before the neighbors could get suspicious about what was going on.

From what she could see through the door viewer, the guy on the other side of the door was tall and thin and dressed in a tuxedo. Royal instantly knew he was there for her and this was some kind of test. She mentally ran through the photos she'd committed to memory of the people in Mancuso's orbit, searching for a match. Leo Rossi, Robert Valentino's cousin.

"We're going to be late if you don't open up."

He didn't sound angry, just like he sincerely didn't want to be late. Royal swung the door wide.

"Cool it," she said. "I've got neighbors who don't want to hear a bunch of commotion."

"Fuck 'em," Leo said. He stuck out his hand. "Leo Rossi. Robert tell you I was picking you up?"

"No."

Leo grinned. "Well, here I am. You gonna invite me in or what?"

Royal wanted to say no, but she knew that answer wouldn't fly. "Thought you said we're going to be late."

"Not too late to have a drink first. Whiskey?"

Royal silently thanked the agents who'd thought to stock the place with alcohol. "Sure." She led the way to the dining room and opened the tall cabinet next to the table. She ignored the more expensive Scotch and pulled down a twelve-year-old bottle of The McCallan and two short heavy glasses. While she poured, she mentally ran through everything she knew about Rossi. He was Robert Valentino's cousin. Not an official employee of Valentino's, but he handled random jobs for Robert. Not a made guy, yet, but definitely interested in taking on more responsibility. Picking her up and keeping an eye on her was likely his contribution to the wedding day. The best thing she could do was to act like his presence was no big deal. She handed him one of the glasses and raised hers in a toast. "To the bride and groom."

"Cheers," Leo said and downed the shot with one gulp. He wiped his lips with the back of his hand. "Good stuff."

She'd been right not to waste the really expensive Scotch on him. "What do you expect? Booze is my thing. You ready to go?"

He looked longingly at the bar, but she didn't offer a refill, partly to retain power and partly because she wasn't interested in having her driver be drunk before they got to the wedding.

"Yeah, we should probably get going."

"Right. Be ready in a sec." Royal left him to process her response and went back to the bedroom to grab her wallet. While she was there she double-checked to make sure the tiny camera stowed in the lapel of her tux was secure and undetectable. Today was going to be a treasure trove of intel, and she needed to capture as much of it as possible. Normally, she'd spend weeks or months building up enough rapport to get an inside track to an event like the Mancuso wedding, and she needed to make the most of the opportunity. She was ready for whatever the day had in store, and if that included seeing Siobhan Collins again, then that was a bonus.

"We got to run an errand on the way," Leo said as he turned off her street.

"No time." Royal pointed at the dashboard clock, fixing her face into a neutral expression to hide the sense of dread creeping up her spine. "I need to make sure things are set up the way I want."

Leo waved her off. "It's cool. Family's going to be at the church for a while. Father Anthony is long-winded." He took the ramp to I-35. "We've got time."

It wasn't cool, but Royal didn't have a lot of options. She

could order him to take her to the Mancuso mansion or she could act nonchalant and play this out. She had a feeling this little detour was a hazing and the best thing she could do was relax into it and act like it was no big deal to go along. "Cool. Show me what you have in mind."

Leo whistled Britney Spears's "Toxic" like he was trying out for a spot on her tour, and Royal squelched her annoyance at his off-key massacre of the tune and settled into dividing her attention between tracking their movements and observing him. From what she remembered from the file, Leo was younger than she was, but he wasn't new to organized crime, having started working for Robert when he was still in high school. Bootlegging seemed so old school, but it was a steady business since alcohol was more stable than real estate when it came to financial investments. Easy, accessible, and the demand crossed all economic lines. While other crime families turned to more trendy enterprises, Mancuso had chosen to invest heavily in businesses that supported his, and booze was at the heart of it.

"You grow up here?"

"In Dallas? No," she lied. "Lived in Houston most of my life, but I'm always open for new opportunities."

"Right. I hear that. Lots of those here if you're willing to put in the work."

Royal heard a slight edge and wondered if he was offering a warning or friendly advice. "How about you? You grow up here?"

"You bet. Played high school ball and everything. You need anything around here, you let me know. I know all the best spots."

A dubious offer for sure. Royal nodded. "Will do."

"We're here." Leo pointed up ahead at a string of warehouses. They were near Harry Hines, and on a Saturday, most of the warehouse fronts were closed. Royal's senses went on high alert as she realized something was about to go down, but she resisted asking any questions, knowing there was a fine line between healthy curiosity and suspicion.

Leo pulled the car up alongside the loading ramp at one of the warehouses and cut the engine. He drummed his fingers on the steering wheel, tapping to the tune that was no longer playing. His hopped-up state was disconcerting, but Royal masked any reaction. She'd expected a test—there was always a test—and the best way to pass was to stay calm. Whatever was about to happen, it was part of the role she was playing, and as long as she stayed in character she'd pass. While she worked this case, she had to sublimate her identity as a cop until she'd gathered enough intel to send the upper echelon of the Mancuso family away for a long, long time. Including Siobhan Collins, no matter how intriguing she might be.

She heard a loud rumble behind them and glanced back to see a semi-trailer pulling into the parking lot, followed by a black Suburban with tinted windows. The truck moved past them, but the SUV pulled up right alongside. Leo's drumming fingers increased their pace, letting her know whoever these people were, their arrival was what he'd been waiting for. She had a feeling she knew what was about to happen. She jerked her chin toward the truck, which was backing up to the loading ramp. "That for us?"

"Damn straight." Leo reached for his door handle. "Come on."

Royal climbed out of the car and followed Leo to the back of the truck where a short, pudgy guy in coveralls was unlocking the rear door. He looked up as they approached, first with a friendly smile then a confused look, likely on account of the fact he wasn't expecting to encounter people in tuxes at one of his regular stops.

"You need something?" he asked.

Leo yanked a gun from his jacket and pointed it at the truck driver. "A few things. How about you step down and have a seat over there." He pointed with his free hand toward the steps that led to the back door of the warehouse. The driver raised his hands in the air and shook his head in disgust. As he walked over to the stairs, four guys stepped out of the Suburban and headed their way. The one in the lead pointed at Royal. "Who's this?"

"Don't worry your pretty head about things that don't concern you," Leo said. He reached into his jacket, pulled out another gun, and handed it to Royal. "You want to watch the driver or the truck?"

Royal reached for the gun, checked the clip, and gestured at the truck. "Like I want to babysit some nobody." She walked toward the open door and motioned for the other guys to follow her. "Let's go."

Careful to keep her tux from catching on anything, she climbed into the back of the truck and glanced around. The rear was stocked with cases of top shelf liquor. She quickly assessed how much they'd need for a three-hundred-person wedding reception and called out orders to the guys from the Suburban, who loaded her selections into the back of their vehicle. When they were done, she jumped down and walked back over to Leo, who was needling the driver about how easy it had been to heist his load.

"We need to go," she said.

"What's the matter?" Leo said. "You scared of getting caught?"

Royal grunted out a laugh. "Not hardly. I'm scared of getting fired." She pointed to her watch. "Reception starts in three hours and I need to be there to oversee the setup. Thirsty guests and no booze? Not going to happen on my watch. Come on."

Leo reached into the truck driver's coveralls and found his phone. He took the SIM card out, tossed it to the ground, and crushed it with his heel. He grabbed the guy by the collar. "You showed up to unload and left the truck to take a piss. When you came back, cases were missing. You didn't see or hear anything. Right?"

The guy's eyes widened, and he nodded slowly.

"Good," Leo said. "There's still plenty in there. You should go ahead and skim a little while you can."

A few minutes later, Royal and Leo were back in the car with the Suburban right behind them. Leo, obviously hopped up after the heist, playfully punched Royal on the arm. "We got some good shit, didn't we?"

"Top shelf," Royal said, injecting her voice with fake enthusiasm she doubted he would notice. "You always get this excited about a job?"

"This wasn't a job. It was a mission. We just snagged the best booze for the boss's daughter's wedding. Kind of a great gift, if you ask me."

She nodded. "Hadn't thought about it that way. Here, I thought you were testing me out."

Leo grinned. "Yeah, well, that too."

She didn't ask if she'd passed since she knew the answer. She encountered folks way scarier than this kid in her long career. If this was the biggest challenge she'd have to face on this job, she'd be very lucky. She only hoped that the close call on the last case hadn't used up all her luck.

CHAPTER SEVEN

Siobhan handed the keys to her Porsche to the valet and walked into the church. She'd ducked Neal's attempts to escort her to the wedding with the excuse that she didn't need a driver or a bodyguard while in the company of the entire Mancuso clan, but she had a feeling she'd be lurking somewhere at the wedding reception in order to keep an eye on her, and because everyone who had any reason to be in the Mancuso orbit today was taking advantage of the opportunity to be part of the grand event.

She was early, but the church was already crowded, and she was relieved to know there would be a seat waiting for her at the front of the sanctuary, and she headed that way.

"Siobhan, can I talk to you for a moment?"

She turned to see the oldest son of the Vedda family standing a few feet away. She hadn't seen Martin in years. It might have been since they were freshmen in college. "Hello. It's good to see you," she said to fill the space.

He smiled. "It's been a long time. I figured you'd be here, but I thought you'd be in the wedding party."

It wasn't the first time someone had mentioned they'd expected Celia to ask her to have a role in the wedding, but people didn't understand that being raised together and having

Carlo Mancuso treat her like a daughter didn't make her an instant sister to Celia and Dominique. Her situation was much more complicated, which was why she was perfectly happy to have a non-matching dress and sit on the sidelines for this charade. If she wanted to make bank off this show, she would've bet against it and raked in. Celia's new husband struck her as the kind of guy who thought he was going to profit from this union not a very auspicious start. "I have other obligations today," she said. "There will be a lot of people who will want to take advantage of the don's happiness today."

He nodded solemnly like they were done talking about silly weddings and were now getting down to business. "I know. Along those lines, I hope we can talk later. I have an exclusive opportunity I'd like to share with you and Don Carlo. An opportunity that could reward any bountiful generosity the don might be feeling on this special day."

"There is a long line in front of you. It will have to be very interesting."

"It is."

Siobhan was used to a bit more fanfare from people trying to get an audience with the don. Supplicants often tried to win her over by saying things like "trust me, it's the greatest thing you'll ever hear," a promise designed to fail. Martin's promise was bold and sure and devoid of flowery promises, and she rearranged her first impression and considered setting up a meet. "Perhaps I will find you later."

She walked off before he could pin her down. She was intrigued, but it wouldn't do to let him think whatever information he had gave him an upper hand. She made her way into the sanctuary and slid into the pew assigned for immediate family just as the strains of the "Wedding March" sounded from the large organ in the balcony and the entire congregation shuffled to their feet.

Celia beamed, all traces of bridezilla gone from her demeanor as she settled into her role as star of the day. Her dress was breathtaking, and she'd likely be featured on the society page as the bride of the year, attention that would only fuel her constant need for attention. Siobhan harbored no envy for she had no desire to be in the spotlight now or at any time. Sometimes she even craved the anonymity of life in a family that wasn't ensnared with complicated relationships and fuzzy lines between what was right for the family versus what was right at all.

After Carlo completed the time-honored act of giving his daughter away like the property she was, he walked back down the aisle and settled into the seat beside her, a signal to any who might be watching of the status she held in the family, whether she was a blood relative or not, lack of a matching dress be damned.

"There will be a lot of business today," he said, his face fixed on the front of the church and his lips barely moving.

"I know. Martin Vedda wants an audience."

"The boy has big ideas."

"Big ideas aren't always bad ideas."

Carlo gave her a subtle nod. It wasn't an agreement to meet with Vedda, but his signal that he'd think about it. She wouldn't push. Pushing had never worked even when she'd been a young child begging for one of the lollipops he used to carry in his jacket pockets for her and his daughters. Carlo Mancuso was the head of the most successful crime family in the region because he had the patience to wait for the best opportunities. When she was younger, she'd viewed his reticence to jump on new ideas as a sign of indecision or being overly cautious, but she'd been wrong. Everything Carlo did was meticulously considered, but he wasn't risk averse. He'd always been willing to risk it all for the right opportunity, but he didn't do so carelessly—a fact that separated him from many of the other organized crime families in Dallas.

After the ceremony, she stayed at the church for a few minutes at Carlo's insistence for a few "family" photos, but she ducked out before the photo shoot ended, knowing Celia didn't want the family lawyer appearing in all of the real family photos. She was fine with the exclusion. Having her picture spread around the society page wasn't a dream of hers, and she preferred to keep a low profile. It was much easier for her to slip in and out of light and dark when she wasn't a local celebrity. She imagined young girls reading the wedding section of the *Dallas Morning News*, oohing and aahing over the featured spread, dreaming of having their own beautiful wedding with no idea of the angst involved behind the scenes.

Back at the Mancuso mansion, Siobhan avoided the crowded valet stand and parked behind the guard house. On the short walk to the house, she ran into Michael, the head of Carlo's security detail, who'd stayed behind to make sure no one entered the grounds who hadn't been invited.

"Good afternoon, Ms. Collins. How was the wedding?"

"It was a beautiful ceremony." She injected the comment with what she hoped was an appropriate amount of awe. He looked at her expectantly, like he wanted to know more, and she dredged up a few more details to placate his interest. "The church was packed. There were lots of beautiful flowers. Father Daniel gave a lovely homily."

"The reception will be nice too," he said with a big smile. "Everything is set up and ready to go. A fairy tale wedding, just like Celia wanted."

Siobhan didn't bother asking Michael how he knew what Celia wanted. He'd had a crush on her since they were in high school together, but he knew Carlo would never permit one of his daughters to marry a man whose sole duty in life was to stand in front of a bullet meant for one of them. She wondered how Carlo would feel if Michael were interested in her instead.

It was a silly question really. While Michael was a catch—handsome, built, and fearless—she craved someone who had the same level of ambition as she did, and Michael was more interested in protecting Carlo's empire than building it bigger and better. Carlo obviously cared deeply about her safety since Neal had beefed up her personal detail since the incident outside of Francine's dress shop. She had spotted Neal's crew following her as soon as she left the church, a sure sign she was important to the family, but she occasionally wondered if her importance was more about the knowledge she had about the family business than any other worth her life might have. It wasn't the first time she'd experienced a tinge of insecurity around her place in the family, and no doubt seeing all the attention centered around one of the real daughters was a splinter niggling its way under her skin today.

"I'll send some cake out for you," she said. "It's going to be a long night. I need you to be extra vigilant. Something's going on, and no one should get in without an invite."

"Always."

He didn't ask any questions, and that both comforted and bothered her. If she ever fell in love, it would be with someone who wanted to know every detail of this life, be in the thick of things, and revel in the details. Though Carlo tried to shield her from the not entirely legal details of his business, that was more about her law license than keeping her in the dark. Besides, she'd never been a perfect soldier, following orders without question and, while she respected such people were necessary, she didn't understand how a person could be wired not to dig deeper.

Siobhan entered the house through the back door that led

to the kitchen. The massive room was whirring with activity, and she paused for a moment to take in the scents and sounds of her childhood.

"Siobhan, come taste this."

She looked across the room at the tall, lean older woman waving a wooden spoon in her direction. Victoria Donovan was the head chef at the Mancuso mansion, and she was strict about who she let into her kitchen, but she'd known Siobhan since childhood and had always welcomed her into this space. She strode over and obediently tasted the spoonful of risotto Victoria placed in her mouth. "Yum, the lemon really brightens it. That's delicious." She ran her tongue around her mouth and closed her eyes. "Tastes familiar."

"It's a variation on your mother's. I'm the only one who knows her exact recipe. Or so she said."

"Then it must be true. Besides, you know she guarded her recipes like gold." Siobhan gripped the edge of the counter as a surge of sentiment rushed through her. For a moment, she was back in time, standing in the kitchen, tugging on her mother's apron and begging her to read her a story, only to be told she had one more thing to do and then she'd be free.

"Her presence lives on, you know."

"I do." But it wasn't the same. Siobhan released her grip and stuffed down the rest of her feelings. "I should go."

"Busy day?"

She heard the tone beneath the words and knew that Victoria meant more than the wedding festivities. All of the staff at the house knew she was the don's confidant, but Victoria seemed to be the only one who realized it was a burden as much as a blessing to be in the inner orbit of such a powerful man. "Yes, but busy is good."

"It is until it consumes you and you come out the other end with no life to show for it." She pointed to the door.

"Weddings aren't simply for the bride and groom, you know. There are lots of eligible prospects here today."

Siobhan smiled to cover her annoyance that Victoria's solution to her getting a life was to find someone else to consume her time and attention. She pointed at the rows of warming trays ready to be filled with the wedding feast. "Speaking of busy, I should go and let you get back to all of this."

She strode off before Victoria could give her another knowing look or a probing gaze. She didn't need her approval and she wasn't sure why she'd sought it. Victoria had been her mother's best friend, but that didn't make her a mother substitute, and she was too old to foolishly pine for parental love.

By the time Siobhan burst through the doors leading to the enormous courtyard where the reception had been staged, she'd placed her emotions back in check, but Victoria's words echoed in her mind. She'd heard the silliness about how everyone cried at weddings and they were the perfect place for connecting with someone else, but all she could think about was she never wanted to be so tied to someone she couldn't break free, and weeping in public was a perfect path to ineptitude.

She spotted one of the many bars and headed that way. A young blonde dressed in a tuxedo shirt smiled broadly and asked what she wanted to drink.

"Jameson. Neat."

The blonde frowned and looked down at the bottles lining her well, pushing some aside and pulling some out to read the labels. "I'm not seeing anything called that."

"You've got to be kidding me." She was more disturbed that this girl didn't know what Jameson was than the fact the bar didn't appear to be stocked with her favorite whiskey.

"I'm sorry, it looks like we don't carry that one."

"Is everything okay here?"

Siobhan turned and locked eyes with Royal. She should've been prepared to see her here after Robert had brought her to the house, and maybe if she'd shown up dressed in jeans and a leather jacket, she would have. But no, today Royal was pulling her best James Bond impression in a tuxedo that looked like it had been custom tailored to her delicious body. She struggled to contain the low growl inching up her throat. "Depends on what you mean by okay. It appears your bartender here has an *almost* fully stocked bar."

Royal's head whipped to the blonde. "What are we missing?"

"Jameson."

Royal stepped behind the bar and nudged the blonde aside. She reached down low, pulled a bottle out, and held it over her head. "One bottle of Irish whiskey, at your service." She handed it to the blonde, stepped out from behind the space, and faced Siobhan. "Anything else I can conjure up for you?"

Siobhan hesitated before responding and let the suggestive retort fizzle into noise of the room. "I'll take that in a glass with a shard of ice," she said, daring Royal to deign to wait on her.

Royal didn't seem fazed by the challenge. She poured three fingers of whiskey into a heavy short glass, cracked an ice cube on the bar, and plucked a sliver and dropped it in the glass. Their fingers touched when she handed it over, and like the first time they'd come into physical contact, the result was electric. Royal motioned to a space a few feet away and Siobhan led the way.

"You look surprised to see me here," Royal said when they were out of the bartender's earshot.

She was surprised, and she shouldn't be since Robert had brought her to the house just the other day. She had personally reviewed the list of vendors, but only to make sure they were supporting the businesses that were loyal to the family, not to check out the names of the individual workers—that she left for Michael. But surprised or not, seeing Royal again was exhilarating. "You'll find I'm rarely surprised. It's my superpower."

"The implication being I will get to spend more time with you in order to be able to recognize this superpower is not a fleeting trait."

Royal's eyes glinted with amusement, and Siobhan knew she should put her in her place, but all she wanted to do was bask in the attention. Royal's focus was different from most of the women she met who were more concerned about bowing and scraping than challenging her. She appreciated the difference, but letting Royal know that would give her too much power. "If you want to spend time with me, you'll have to find a way to become indispensable." She held up her glass. "Some way besides locating the missing Jameson."

"Goals." Royal grinned. "I can work with that. Now, if you'll excuse me, I'm going to personally recheck all of the bar setups to make sure your favorite whiskey is readily available." She took a step away, but then stopped and turned back, pointing at the drink in Siobhan's hand. "If you need another, though, I hope you'll find me so I can give you a perfect pour."

Her eyes smoldered on those last words and Siobhan was certain "pour" was code for more. A lot more. Siobhan watched Royal's back as she walked away, and for a second, she was tempted to tell her to stay, but she didn't have time to indulge her personal fantasies today, and this place was too public for her to let down her guard.

She downed the rest of her drink, set the glass on a nearby table, and glanced around the reception. The tents had filled with wedding guests and the revelry was well underway. Celia and Tony had just entered the room and were about to have their first dance, after which she would duck out and head to the don's office for the first of many meetings the shield of this social event allowed him to have without the danger of being observed by the federal agents who constantly dogged their business.

She watched the ostensibly happy couple skate across the dance floor, Celia looking like a butterfly and Tony like a caterpillar not quite ready to come out of its chrysalis, and she predicted Tony wasn't going to last long in the overpowering presence of Celia, who would pose as the doting wife but would dominate his every move with her status as the don's daughter, and her desire to curate her life to fit the picture she'd painted for herself. The pressure from his new wife would be as daunting as the pressure he would have to perform as the newest member of the Mancuso family. Part of her job today would be to introduce him to his new role.

"The don is ready for you," Neal whispered in her ear. "And thanks for not losing us on the way back here from the church."

"I'm saving my race car driving skills for a day I can really be alone. Today is not that day. Let's start with Tony before he gets too deep into the bourbon. Give me ten minutes with the don and bring him up."

She edged away from the crowd and walked back into the house, avoiding the kitchen and the memories it held. But as she made her way up the back staircase, she spotted the linen closet on the landing and remembered spending an hour behind the door, in the dark, while she waited for Dominique and Celia to find her. She'd been too young and naive to realize they would never come looking for her near the servants' quarters, but her mother had explained that no matter how close she and the Mancuso girls might be, there would be times when their worlds would diverge, and she would be left on the outside.

"Which is why you have to be strong and fearless, cara. *It's the only way to survive in this world. You make decisions based on survival, and you hope that someday you'll be safe and secure."*

Years later, Siobhan remembered her mother's words, the way her eyes flashed with determination when she spoke them and the firm cadence of her voice. She'd vowed then to heed the advice though she hadn't fully understood what she meant. She knew now.

She shook her head to clear away the memories and gripped the stair rail. She'd taken another step when she heard a voice call her name, and she glanced over her shoulder to see Royal standing a few feet away looking at her with a curious expression. "Shouldn't you be working?"

"I'm always working," Royal said, "but sometimes I'm working somewhere new, which means I don't always know where I'm going." She shrugged, her expression sheepish. "I seem to be lost."

Siobhan spent a moment analyzing Royal's words before she decided they were genuine. Besides, she knew better than most how easy it was to get lost in this house. She pointed down the stairs. "Down one flight and take the hallway to your left. It'll lead you to a door that exits the side of the house and you'll be back at the party."

Royal nodded slowly. "And what about you?"

Siobhan smiled. "I'm not lost."

A flicker of something crossed Royal's face and she closed her eyes for a moment, like she was thinking. When she opened them, she returned the smile. "I suppose I need to get back to the party." She turned and started to walk back down the stairs.

Siobhan watched her go. One step, two steps…By the sixth step she couldn't resist the urge to call her back. "Wait."

Royal turned slowly and met her eyes. "Yes?"

"Come with me." She stared at Royal, willing her to not ask questions, to trust whatever she had in store. Most people who worked in the don's orbit would jump at the chance to do whatever his consigliere asked, but Royal took a moment before responding, which made Siobhan both curious and respectful.

"My pleasure," Royal said. She flourished her arm. "Lead the way."

CHAPTER EIGHT

Royal's heart pounded as she followed Siobhan up another flight of stairs, but it had nothing to do with the exertion of the climb. Where was Siobhan taking her? Siobhan had a reputation for assignations, but part of that reputation was not repeating the same act with the same woman, which could be a problem if they were headed toward an intimate meeting right now. She'd have to either find a way to delicately wriggle out of the situation or give in and convince Siobhan she wasn't her typical fare in order to stay close enough to do her job. Wharton never should've whored her out on this job without a safety net, and she added this "favor" to the long list of reasons she was ready to be done with undercover work.

They reached the top of the stairway and turned to the left on the wide landing. Royal shot a quick look to the right and noted there was a door at each end of the hallway and one in the middle. From what she could tell from the outside of the house, this third story was about half the size of the two floors below. She shifted her initial impression that Siobhan might be taking her to a bedroom because she had a hunch these rooms, strategically placed in the compound, were the operation center of the Mancuso family business. When they reached the door at the end of the hallway, Siobhan placed her hand on the knob and looked back at her.

"Are you ready?"

The question was deceptively simple, but without knowing for sure what was behind the door, Siobhan had the upper hand. Royal suspected she usually did. She mustered the kind of swagger she knew was expected from anyone who was interested in rising in the ranks and said, "I've never been more ready."

Siobhan eased the door open and held up a hand at the large man standing on the other side. He wasn't visibly armed, but considering his size, he didn't need to be, and it was pretty clear he was a gatekeeper. Royal followed Siobhan through the doorway and looked around. She'd been expecting to be standing in a room, but this was an entryway, a fake entrance of sorts, leading to another door a few feet away.

"Is he alone?" Siobhan asked.

"Waiting for you," the man answered. He pointed at Royal. "Who's this?"

"New business."

Royal watched the exchange, noting Siobhan's confidence—very sexy—and the easy way she smacked down his question. The dynamics were interesting and exactly the kind of thing she was here to observe. The allure of Siobhan wielding her power was a total bonus.

The man stepped aside, and Siobhan opened the second door a crack, but before she swung it wide, she fixed Royal with a look and placed a finger over her lips. Royal nodded to show she understood and then followed her into the room where Don Carlo Mancuso, dressed in a tuxedo, sat behind a giant desk.

She'd expected to see Carlo today, at the wedding reception, but not this close and not this privately. Her gut clenched a little at the idea her identity might've been discovered, and she mentally recounted everything that had happened so far that day from the moment Leo had picked her up at the house to the heist at the semi this afternoon. Instinctively, she hung back while Siobhan strode confidently to the desk.

"Siobhan," Carlo said, taking both of her hands into his. "I hear you have declined your detail. Tell me that's not true."

Siobhan laughed. "I guess I better stop trusting Neal to keep my secrets. No, they still follow me everywhere, but I wanted to drive myself today. I haven't had much of a chance to enjoy your very generous gift since things have heated up."

Royal took note of the easy affection and informal discourse between Carlo and Siobhan. She was indeed like a daughter to him, but with her law degree and position as consigliere, ten times more powerful.

"Would you like to introduce me to this new person before we move on to other matters?"

Despite the inflection, it wasn't a question, and Royal watched with interest to see how Siobhan handled the command.

"Carlo Mancuso, I'd like to introduce Royal Flynn." Siobhan motioned for her to come closer. "She's working with Robert."

"Yet here she is with you. Who is taking care of our guests?" Carlo asked.

Royal paused mid-step. "It's an honor to meet you. I assure you, sir, everything is going well, but you're right. I should get back to the reception." She bowed slightly and started to back away.

"No, stay," Siobhan said, holding up a hand before turning back to Mancuso. "Royal is the one who saved my life last week. Without regard for her own safety."

"And she believes she is owed a reward for this favor?" Carlo asked.

Siobhan met her eyes before turning back to Carlo. "No, she doesn't. In fact, she hasn't mentioned it again. But I believe she has earned a chance to prove she can be of even more value to the family." She turned back to Royal. "You're not averse to taking on more work, are you?"

"Not averse at all," Royal replied, knowing there was only one answer.

Carlo interlocked his fingers and studied Siobhan, his face devoid of expression, as was hers. Royal watched the silent yet meaningful exchange between them, curious about the fact they spoke as if she wasn't in the room and wondering how often Siobhan pressed a point with Mancuso. Judging by his surprise she was doing so now, she figured it wasn't often, and it was cheeky to risk outright rejection in front of a practical stranger. Royal filed the fact away with the many other random bits of information she'd gathered about this secretive family and vowed to sort it all out later.

"Come closer, please."

Royal snapped to attention and followed Carlo's command, but she waited to speak until she heard what he had to say, taking the time to notice, now that she was closer to him, that he was pale and his hands trembled slightly. Was he ill?

"I owe you a debt of gratitude for saving the life of someone I hold dear. You wish to redeem this debt by working for me?"

Royal kept her voice calm and even. "I could think of no greater honor than to be in your service." The cloying words were thick and hard to swallow, but she did her best to sell the deference she didn't feel.

Carlo patted the desk. "Very well. We will find a place

where you can do well. For both of us. Siobhan will discuss the details with you later."

Siobhan caught Royal's gaze and offered a hint of a smile. Royal desperately wanted to stick around, but she was certain Carlo's words had been a polite dismissal. "Thank you, Don. Royal, we'll talk later," Siobhan said, her tone making it clear they were done for now.

Royal nodded and started toward the door, but before she reached it, it flew open and a tall, gorgeous woman she instantly recognized as Dominique entered the room.

"Well, well, well. Who is this tall, gorgeous specimen?" Dominique said. She downed a half-full champagne glass, set it down, and stopped to run her hand along the edge of Royal's lapel. "I don't believe we've met," she said, her voice a smooth purr.

Royal felt the heat of Siobhan's glare from across the room. She wanted to tell her not to worry, she was the target of her supposed affections, but instead she leaned into the attention from Dominique, sensing any conflict that might arise from being at the center of this faux sibling rivalry might prove interesting. She'd learned a long time ago to look for wedges anywhere she could find them and exploit when necessary. She stuck out her hand. "Royal Flynn, nice to meet you." By now she was able to deliver her phony last name smoothly.

"Poppa, you're supposed to have security that blends into the background. This one won't do at all, though I suppose there's some value in having someone this distractingly good-looking on the clock." She ran a hand down Royal's arm. "I may have to steal this one for my own."

Royal balked at Dominique's objectifying language, but she played the role of dutiful servant and didn't speak or otherwise react to Dominique's touch. She did take in the piercing glare in Siobhan's eyes and knew Dominique had gotten a rise out of her even as she tried to squelch any display of an emotional response.

"Dominique, we have business to discuss."

Siobhan's voice was sharp and commanding, but Dominique didn't fall in line. Instead she leaned close and whispered in Royal's ear. "I'll find you later."

Royal took the cue and strode toward the door, taking care to appear indifferent about being dismissed, but inwardly wishing she had a valid reason to stay, certain that the underbelly of the Mancuso criminal empire would be conducting all kinds of business this day judging by how many notables from other crime families she'd seen at the reception so far. But as she left the room, she couldn't deny the thing she was going to miss the most was the opportunity to be in the presence of the enigmatic Siobhan, and she hoped that "later" would come soon.

❖

"Who was that?"

Siobhan wished Dominique would keep her mouth shut, but years of hoping she would be more discreet had only convinced her wishing was futile. "Royal is working with Robert, but we're considering giving her more responsibility."

"Has she been checked out?" Dominique asked. "Or is looking delicious our new criteria for promotion?"

"She handled a run today like she'd done it dozens of times before. Not to mention she saved my life before she even knew there was anything to gain by doing so." Siobhan crossed her arms to signal the conversation was over, knowing that with Dominique it never really was. Fast friends as kids, the two of them had learned to trust each other as adults, but only because Carlo expected them to work in tandem. As they'd grown older, their interests had diverged, and they were constantly testing the power balance between them. Siobhan knew every decision both of them made was for the good of the family, but increasingly, they had very different ideas of how to define their goals. She was careful and calculating where Dominique was bold and brash, taking on unnecessary risk. So far, Dominique's methods had yielded crazy profits, but her strategies were the reason Jimmy had wound up being arrested by the feds, and if she kept up her current trajectory, she could very well endanger the inner circle of the Mancuso family. That Dominique would question Royal when she so easily embraced risk in every other aspect of the family business was laughable, and Siobhan was certain it was because bringing Royal on hadn't been her idea in the first place.

Hell, she questioned her own judgment around Royal. What was it about this woman that threatened her composure whenever they were in the same room? Sure, Royal was strong and good-looking, and those piercing eyes were mesmerizing, but she had her pick of many similarly beautiful women. Maybe it was Royal's nonchalance. The women Siobhan usually met, whether for a quick lay or an actual date, were all more interested in her role in the family versus her as an individual, but from the first moment they'd met, with Royal hurtling herself between her and the oncoming SUV, she'd known Royal was different. They hadn't known each other at all then, but in that moment, by her actions, Siobhan knew more about Royal than any background check or date night conversation could reveal, and she trusted her now because of it. Careless? Perhaps, but her instincts were her most trusted resource and they'd served her well thus far.

"Speaking of saving lives, has anyone figured out who tried to run down our little Shiv?"

Dominique addressed the question to Carlo, but it was

clearly designed to get a rise out of her and she wasn't going to take the bait. "I think it was Petrov's people. They haven't been happy since we cut ties last month. We delivered the message, so they delivered one back."

Siobhan was skeptical. It was true—they had stopped doing business with the Russians when they'd learned the events they'd catered for them that were supposed to be a cover for a mutual bootlegging operation and money laundering scheme were also being used as a wholesale prostitution ring. The Mancusos' enterprises consisted of mostly illegal activities, but they drew the line at human trafficking in any form. "Maybe it was Petrov, but I'd expect a more personalized message if it was. A random drive-by doesn't seem like his style."

"I think it's exactly the kind of thug move the Russians would make, and I think they're also responsible for the nuisance hits we've been taking—the thefts, the poor reviews. Sitting around and letting them get away with this stuff signals weakness," Dominique said. "It's time to deliver a decisive message in return."

"What do you want to do?" Siobhan asked. "Tail them and run down every higher-up in the family? You'll start an all-out war."

Dominique shook her head. "They'll back off at the first sign of strength. They don't have the stomach for a real fight."

"No telling how many lives you'll risk testing that theory. Mikhail Petrov is a reasonable man. I suggest a sit-down before things escalate out of control," Siobhan said.

"Waste of time. Besides, who's going to do it?"

Carlo held up a hand to signal the conversation was over. "A meeting is a good idea, but he hasn't earned the right to sit down with me. Siobhan, set it up and convey to him my deepest desire for a truce."

Siobhan heard the coded language and knew she was

being tasked with convincing the Petrovs that if they didn't
stand down, they would go down, and sending her when she'd
been the object of their violence was a signal the Mancusos
were fearless. Her task would be complicated by the fact
she'd be showing up to a meeting of a family head without the
power balance of the Mancuso don, but she was up for it and
grateful Carlo hadn't decided to assign Dominique to join her.
"I'll take care of it."

"What other business do you two have for me today?"

"Martin Vedda would like to talk to you about a business
opportunity. I think you should hear him out."

"More of his family's old-fashioned, outdated 'opportunities'?" Dominique asked, using air quotes to signal her opinion
about Martin's business plan. "Why is he coming to us?"

"Because it's not outdated, and his own family can't
sustain what he has planned. Be glad he's coming to us instead
of one of the other families."

"He still sweet on you?"

Siobhan shrugged off the needling. "It's business, D. Let
it go."

"It's always business with you. Poppa, tell Siobhan she
needs a more well-rounded life."

"If I wanted to hear you girls bicker, I'd tell you so.
Focus, please." He motioned to Siobhan. "What is this new
business that's so ambitious the Veddas can't sustain it without
our help?"

"I'd prefer to let him explain it to you." She waited,
fairly certain he would grant her this request, but as always
trepidatious about trusting his favor.

"Fine. Bring him in."

Siobhan motioned to the guard at the door and hoped
Martin had shown up outside as she'd asked. She needn't

have worried. He was right outside the door, pacing. "Are you practicing for a marathon?"

"Very funny." He pointed at the door. "Is he ready to hear my idea?"

"Certainly," Siobhan said. "You'll have fifteen minutes, including questions."

"Generous," he muttered under his breath, but loud enough for her to hear.

"I have a long list of people who would give up half their fortune for such a slot. If you don't want it, let me know and I'll move on." Siobhan waited a moment and then started walking back toward the door.

"Wait."

She stopped but didn't turn.

"I want to talk to him."

She glanced over her shoulder. "Come on, then." She pushed through the door while he scampered to catch up. Dominique was now sitting on the sofa to the side of Carlo's desk and she'd switched from Champagne to a martini.

"Is this Mr. Big Idea?" Dominique said with a hint of a slur. "Hey, what's the big idea?"

She laughed at her own joke, while the rest of the room was uncomfortably silent. Siobhan saw the flash of disappointment cross Carlo's face before he motioned to Martin. If Dominique would keep her act together, she was destined to one day run the Mancuso empire, and Siobhan would never understand why that wasn't a superior motivation to keep it together. In the meantime, it was up to her to keep things on track. She made the introductions. "Don Carlo, Martin would like to discuss a business opportunity. I informed him you have granted fifteen minutes of your time to hear what he has to say," she said in case Martin tried to overstep.

Carlo rolled his hand at Martin, signaling him to begin.

Martin punched a few buttons on his phone and held it up to display an app. "Liquor delivery. Not long-haul trucks from wholesale to retail, but delivered by rideshare, direct from the wholesaler to the consumer."

"Already being done," Dominique blurted out.

"Not really," Martin said.

"What makes your app special?" Siobhan asked. "I get emails from a half dozen others touting their service."

"Everyone offers two-hour delivery or even same day service, but the one thing none of them do is deliver direct from wholesale."

"And?" Dominique asked.

Martin grinned like he'd been waiting for someone to ask him that very question. "And the result is every other app relies on the inventory of retailers over which they have no control. By delivering direct from a wholesaler like say, Valentino's, you would have complete control over your inventory. Plus, you can track consumer sales so you know what to stock. You can underprice everyone else on the market because you're cutting out the middleman, and you'll run the books on the backend."

Siobhan would swear he winked at that last statement, but the gesture was so subtle, she couldn't be sure. "Who owns the app? I mean right now." She wanted to know who in the Vedda family she'd need to get to sign off before they made a commitment.

"I own the program. The copyright is already registered, and it's ready to be licensed."

Siobhan started to say if they were going in business with him, they wouldn't be licensing his app, they'd own it outright. Carlo wasn't big on owning things that weren't tangible, but she decided it was best to iron out the details after Carlo decided whether he was interested at all.

Dominique and Carlo spent the balance of the fifteen minutes asking Martin more questions and then Siobhan escorted him out of the room. She motioned to Michael, who was waiting outside. Michael nodded at her and held out his hand for Martin's phone.

"What?" Martin's eyes narrowed, clutching his phone to his chest.

"He's going to check your phone," Siobhan said, "give him your password." She hoped Martin wasn't stupid enough to ask why. She watched while Michael scrolled through Martin's photos and checked for recordings. He handed the phone back to Martin, but addressed his comments to her. "It's clean."

Martin tucked the phone in his jacket pocket, obviously agitated at the search, but it was standard operating procedure for anyone who had a meeting with the don unless they were made men. It struck her she'd neglected to subject Royal to the search, and she cursed how easily she'd let herself be distracted by Royal's charm and good looks. She couldn't let that happen again.

"Do you think he's interested?" Martin asked.

Siobhan tore her attention back to the business at hand. She'd seen Carlo's wheels turning with ideas about how to incorporate Martin's app plan into his empire, but she kept her poker face fixed in place. "I'll let you know."

"You have until Wednesday and then I'm taking this elsewhere."

She sighed. "You know better than that. Don Carlo will not be pushed into a decision, and if you really want to get this business up and running, we are your best bet. You'll wait until he makes a decision and you'll be grateful for the opportunity." She kept her tone even and didn't raise her voice, but the sharp rebuke landed as it should. He nodded and shook her hand.

"I'll look forward to your call. I think we would do well in business together, you and me."

She didn't bother correcting him as he walked away, having no desire to give any oxygen to his implication that she might be remotely interested in his affections. There was a time when she would try anything, but people like Martin might say they were interested in one-night stands, but they were really only interested in finding the one, and she would never be that. Not for him, not for anyone.

Her mind strayed to Royal. If she was inclined to fool around today, Royal would be more her style—or she would've been before she was under Mancuso employ. Siobhan steered away from entanglements with employees, making a rare exception for some of the temporary help around the house. But Royal wasn't like those women. She had a depth to her, a quiet strength that spoke of layers and layers to peel away. A woman like that wasn't usually inclined to fuck and move on. Or maybe she was worried *she* wouldn't be able to fuck and move on. Either way, steering clear of Royal was her plan, and when she made a plan, she held fast. There was no other way to survive.

CHAPTER NINE

Royal heard her phone buzzing, but the room was dark, and she couldn't find it. She shuffled all the pillows out of the way until she found it in between the sheets, fished it out, and mumbled "Royal here."

"'Bout time you answered. What's going on?"

Royal groaned inwardly at the sound of Wharton's voice and sat up in bed. "I was sleeping."

"It's after ten. Seriously?"

"I was out late. On a job." She glanced around, hesitating to say more. She knew how to sweep a room for bugs and she'd done so regularly since she'd moved in, but you could never be too careful. "You know how much I hate talking on the phone."

"Meet me for coffee. The usual place."

She didn't want to meet him. She didn't want to meet anyone. She wanted to hole up in this place, away from her boss, the Mancuso family, her brother, and start a completely new life where she was Royal Scott, a person with one identity and a whole lot less baggage to bring to whatever new experiences she might encounter.

Experiences...Her mind flashed to Siobhan Collins and she squelched the thought. Siobhan wasn't a path toward breaking free from this twilight zone life she'd been leading. No, her attraction to Siobhan threatened to have her running back into the fire, full force. The chemistry between them should help her do her job, but if she wasn't careful, she risked getting burned in more ways than one. She needed to get a handle on her feelings before they led her astray. "I'll see you at noon," she said, choosing a busy time for the popular cafe.

She padded her way to the kitchen, brewed a pot of coffee, and spread her notes out on the kitchen table. The wedding had been a goldmine of who's who in the world of organized crime, but except for the private meetings in Don Carlo's office, no one seemed to be discussing business. She'd diligently worked the floor, hoping to overhear anything at all about any big moves the Mancuso family might be up to, but she came up empty on every pass. The conversations generally consisted of nothing more than the indulgent gossip of the rich and privileged. She now knew plenty about the personal relationships between the families, and she might be able to put that information to good use, but there'd been no bombshells, no earth-shattering revelations—not that she'd expected any, but it would've been nice to walk away with some nugget she could mine further.

It had been five days and she'd heard zip from Siobhan. "I'll find you later" had been a promise unfulfilled and she'd barely seen Siobhan the rest of the day other than from a distance, across the room. The day after the wedding, she'd gone to the office and met with Robert, run the liquor inventory, and helped cook the books for the booze they'd stolen from the truck on Celia's wedding day, but she didn't have much intel for her efforts.

When she'd finished the last of the coffee, she swept her notes, locked them in a plain metal box, and stowed them back in the attic. It was definitely a risk to keep them on hand, but she needed the visual of seeing all the bits of information displayed in front of her in order to be able to arrange the pieces of the puzzle as they fell into place. Some undercover agents preferred to encrypt everything on their phones, but no method was completely safe. Besides, she could burn paper notes, but completely eliminating a digital footprint was a more difficult task.

The coffee shop was two miles away, but she chose to walk since she didn't put it past the Mancusos to put a tracker on her car. When she arrived, she circled the place several times to detect if anyone was following or watching her or Wharton, who she could see sitting at the counter, nursing a cup of coffee. Satisfied she'd taken all the appropriate precautions, she went inside, took a seat next to him, and ordered an iced tea and a roast beef sandwich.

"How are you?" he asked when the waitress disappeared into the kitchen.

"Starving. Your people stocked the fridge with crap. Maybe have them check with a person first to see what they actually eat before wasting time."

"Okay. Any other complaints?"

"Sorry. It's been days since the wedding, and despite their promise to elevate me, I haven't heard from anyone. I saw Robert on Sunday and again last night for another take down of an incoming liquor delivery, but other than an attagirl for zeroing out the cost of booze for the reception, it's been crickets. I'm either blown or they're just not interested."

"When did you get to be so impatient? You know jobs like this take time."

"And you assured me they were teed up to do something big soon. I don't have a clue what that something is, and I seriously doubt I'm going to figure it out anytime soon." She slid an index card across the bar. "That's a list of everyone

I saw at the wedding and a chart showing the relationships between them along with my other notes. It's not a lot, but it does fill in a few gaps in the intel you had before. I'm in until the rest of the week and if nothing shakes out, I'm done."

"Really? You're going to give up so easily?"

She knew better than to offer empty threats. As much as she wanted to walk away from this life, she was hooked enough to want to see this through. If only she could find a way to accelerate her investigation, but jobs like this didn't work that way. Normally, she'd spend months laying the groundwork before she could develop hard evidence. The difference was that unlike after every other job, after the last one, she'd expected to be done. And then there was the issue of her brother showing up at her apartment and the mystery about his arrival having to wait. "Tell you what. Do me a favor and I'll stick around, but how long remains to be seen." She gave him Ryan's military info and he promised to look into it and report back.

"So, what's she like?" he asked as he stowed the index card in his jacket.

"Who?" She knew who, but she felt a strange reluctance to talk about Siobhan.

"The consigliere. It always surprised me that Carlo didn't pick Dominique for the job and went outside the family."

"She seems like family." Royal reflected on the way Siobhan and Carlo had interacted, the doting father figure and the attentive daughter. "Dominique is pretty brash. Maybe he thinks Siobhan has a cooler head for giving counsel."

"You could be right about that. They say Siobhan's like a daughter to him."

Royal pictured the way Siobhan had placed her hand on Carlo's arm, establishing a connection as she entreated him to find a better job for her in the family business. But maybe the appearance was greater than the real thing since, days later, she'd heard nothing from the Mancusos about coming into the fold. "Something like that."

"You need to get into her place, at the very least her office."

"So now you're telling me how to do my job?"

"She's the key."

"And she's a lawyer. You really want me poking around her office? You won't be able to use anything I get." She took a drink of her coffee. "Has main Justice signed off on you targeting a lawyer?"

He shifted in his chair. "We're not targeting her. Not officially. Listen, you find something juicy and I'll figure out how we can use it. Trust me, I got this."

Like every other time in her life, when she heard the words "trust me," Royal's internal alarm system started going off. After years working with him, she had grown to trust Wharton, but now she wondered how much of her trust was about survival rather than good sense. Going after lawyers was sensitive business in the federal system. They couldn't be indicted without the blessing of the Department of Justice, and that usually resulted only after evidence had been gathered, not the other way around. What Wharton was talking about was bootstrapping the evidence to fit the supposition, something she didn't mind doing when there was some imminent danger, but in a case like this where they were doing run-of-the-mill catch-a-gangster investigations, it didn't make sense to risk guilty verdicts with unnecessary technical violations. Slow and steady old-school investigation would yield results—they always did.

And apparently, she'd just talked herself out of bailing too soon. "I'll let you know what I find," she said, hedging against an outright promise to toss Siobhan's office, but his suggestion did spark an idea. She pushed her cup away and stood. "Next time, wait for me to call you." She took a step toward the door before she remembered what she'd been planning to ask him. "Hey, is Carlo ill?"

"Not that I know of, why?"

She remembered the signs she'd seen. He'd been pale and shaky, but she'd been pale and shaky after a long night at the bar. It was probably just stress from the wedding. Weddings were usually happy events in memory only. "No reason. Never mind."

She took a different route on the walk home, stopping at a used bookstore. She missed the shelves of books at her apartment, a collection she hadn't added much to in a while. She ran her hands along the spine of the last Sue Grafton book before returning it to the shelf. Buying certain titles said something about who a person was, and she couldn't risk the message they might send. So, when she was working undercover, she bought books she thought would best reflect the role she was trying to play. Sometimes they overlapped with the books she'd choose on her own, but often not. Today, she picked up a conspiracy theory book about how the government was a sham and people shouldn't have to pay income tax. Pretty fringe, but still a bestseller so she could use it to either claim credibility with the people who were anti-government or claim curiosity with those that were more moderate. She paid for the book, waved off the offer of a bag, tucked it under her arm, and continued her walk. She was about a quarter mile from her place when her phone rang, caller unknown.

"Yeah," she said, answering the call.

"Where are you?"

She recognized Siobhan's silky voice and recalibrated. She'd been formulating a plan to drop in at her office with some made-up legal need, but Siobhan reaching out to her was a much better development. "Out for a walk in my neighborhood. Where are you?"

"Hold on."

Royal waited a few moments and then held the phone away from her ear to see if the line was still connected. When she heard Siobhan's voice come through again, she pulled it back to her ear. "What was that?"

"Turn around."

She turned slowly, cautious about the fact she'd been walking without a lot of regard to what was going on around her. It only took a moment to spot the black Suburban at the end of the block headed her way. If that was Siobhan, this was next-level surveillance, and she wondered if they'd seen her at the cafe. She shook her head. No, Siobhan had seemed genuinely curious when she'd asked where she was.

She stood in place and watched the vehicle approach, acting nonchalant when the rear window lowered to reveal Siobhan.

"Get in."

It was another test of her ability and willingness to do whatever they said without question, and for a second, she thought back to her days in the military where she'd spent a lot of time balking at jumping through hoops like these. Was Ryan having similar issues and was that why he was on an indefinite leave? She shelved the question for later and climbed into the SUV. The seats in the back were arranged like the passenger section of a limo with two rows facing each other, and she took the seat opposite Siobhan. She was barely seated when Siobhan told the driver, the bodyguard Royal recognized from the day she'd pushed Siobhan out of the street, to go.

"How are you today?" Siobhan asked, her tone formal.

"Good. Went out for a walk, had coffee, and checked out

the local bookstore." Royal held up the book and then tucked it back under her arm.

"I didn't picture you as the type of person who indulged conspiracy theories."

"I read all kinds of things. Nothing wrong with covering all your bases."

"Why aren't you working today?"

Royal stifled a reaction to the quick change in subject and went with the flow. "Robert told me not to come in. Said he'd call me later."

"So, this gives you time to read and you choose to use it on nonsense."

"Nonsense?"

"Those books all rail against the bureaucracy of government, but only because they want a different kind of government. One that reflects only their ideas. The authors are hypocrites."

Royal sensed a well of emotion from Siobhan about this issue and she played on it. "Wow, tell me how you really feel."

"Tell me you don't believe everything you read."

"I don't believe much I can't sort out for myself. Not to worry, I'm in no danger of joining up with the fringe right. I'm more of a live and let live kind of person." She waited, but Siobhan didn't respond, so she pushed a little more. "How about you?"

"How about me what?"

"You don't strike me as someone who likes to be told what to do."

"You'd be right about that." Siobhan studied her carefully. "You don't strike me as someone who grew up thinking they were going to peddle alcohol for the rest of her life."

"Ouch." Royal paused for a moment to consider the source of the comment. Did Siobhan already suspect she was hiding something or was the comment more of a backhanded compliment? Treading carefully, she said, "You make it sound so low-rent."

Siobhan waved her hand dismissively. "Sorry. I'm not saying it's not an important job, but…Never mind."

"No way. Now I'm curious. What exactly do you think I should be doing?"

The SUV pulled to a stop at the intersection. "Good question. You're definitely a person who steps up. I guess I wonder how you got started working for someone like Robert."

"Well, now you have me curious about exactly what you think of Robert."

"And you think I'd trust you enough to share my opinion?"

"You seem full of opinions and you haven't been shy about sharing them yet."

"Why don't *you* tell me what you think of him. Bonus points for honesty."

Royal studied Siobhan's face, looking for some clue about whether this conversation was idle gossip or a test. Either way, both the questions and answers could be revealing both for her and Siobhan. She took a deep breath and plunged ahead. "Robert is ambitious. Becoming a made member of the Mancuso family is his dream and he can't think of anything more fulfilling in life."

"Now it's my turn to point out that you say that like it's a bad thing."

Royal shook her head. "It's not. The problem is that, as far as he's concerned, the goal is more important than the getting there. He'll do anything to suck up to Don Carlo, and the anything may not always be in the family's best interest."

"And you profess to know what's in the Mancuso family's best interest?"

"Not entirely, but Carlo Mancuso's reputation is that he

values both loyalty and discretion. Robert may seem loyal, but his loyalty comes with a price. If he doesn't escalate through the ranks, he's the kind of person who will turn. And as for discretion? You've seen how he struts around. He likes to brag just to let people know he's on the inside without regard to what being on the inside really means."

"He's your boss."

"You asked me a question. I'm merely answering."

"Or maybe you're trying to undermine Robert. Maybe you think there's a chance if he doesn't get a seat at the table there might be room for you someday."

"I thought you had decided I wasn't ambitious."

"I'm not afraid to admit when I'm wrong."

Royal grinned. "I doubt that happens very often."

Siobhan grinned back. "Hardly ever." The light changed and the driver pulled out into the intersection. "Let's see how ambitious you are. Do you have plans Friday night?"

Royal didn't have a clue if there was an event planned because Robert hadn't called her since the wedding. She knew how these guys worked and he'd probably try to spring something on her at the last minute, but as of right now, she was completely free and she said so.

"Perfect," Siobhan said. "Pick me up at seven. I'll text you the address." The SUV pulled up to Royal's house and parked by the curb. "See you then."

Royal wanted to ask a bunch of questions but sensed this whole car ride had been a test and it would continue until she stepped out of the car. She reached for the door handle and gave it a yank. She had one foot out of the car when Siobhan placed a hand on her arm. Gently, but with confident force. Royal turned back and locked eyes with her. "Yes?"

"Friday night is black tie. Is that a problem?"

Royal flashed her a broad smile. "Nope. Looking forward to it."

A moment later, she stood on the sidewalk and watched the SUV speed away. She had no idea what she'd be doing with her Friday night, but she couldn't wait to see her. Even if she had to wear a tux again.

CHAPTER TEN

Siobhan reached into her safe and located the flash drive Dominique had given her with last week's numbers, and she used it to back up the reports she'd promised Carlo, making sure to encrypt the files. When the backup was complete, she stowed the drive in her bag before signing out of her computer. It had been a long week and all she wanted to do was go home, pour a deep glass of whiskey, and tuck into a long, hot bath.

No such luck. Tonight was the annual donors' gala at the Dallas Museum of Art, and she'd been tasked with serving as the public face of the Mancuso family to accept an award for their generous donations. Carlo had asked Dominique to attend in his place, but D had made up some excuse about having to meet with some potential investors. Siobhan was certain she'd timed the meeting to avoid having to schmooze with a bunch of high society types who likely thought she was only at the event because of the family donation.

Siobhan didn't have any interest in schmoozing either, but she was used to being left to shoulder any jobs Dominique wasn't in the mood to handle, and this was no different. The only saving grace was she would have a striking woman on her arm, which would save her from being the target of Dallas's other eligible bachelors and bachelorettes during the course of the evening.

She wondered what Royal was doing right now. Was she already dressed and in her car headed this way or was she still fiddling with her tie and the buttons on her vest? Putting her on the spot for a black-tie event had been kind of mean, but it was a good way to test Royal's ambition, not to mention see her in evening wear again. She pictured her standing on the landing at the Mancuso mansion. Tall, handsome, rakish…

No, no, no. She needed to stop thinking about Royal in any capacity other than what she could do to help the family business. Besides, she wasn't in the habit of indulging her desires with anyone in the close family orbit and she wasn't about to start now—not when she needed to stay focused to deal with whatever trouble was headed their way. She shoved her phone and laptop into her bag, stood, and walked to the door. Like a mind reader, Neal was waiting in the lobby, and she gave her a small wave.

"How do you always know when I'm ready to leave?"

She shrugged. "It's not that hard. You have the gala tonight and I know you like to take a little extra time to get ready for fufu events."

Was she that predictable? She supposed it was true. She did have a tendency to leave work earlier than usual when she had to attend a gala, and tonight she would need to speak as well. Funny how she had absolutely no trouble being a boss in the courtroom, but when it came to mixing it up with Dallas's high society, her stomach rumbled, and she scrambled to silence the voice inside whispering how she didn't belong.

And she didn't belong. Not really. The only way the Mancuso family was able to rub shoulders with the rest of the Dallas elite was because they bought their way in with charitable donations. A new hospital wing, a campus library, the donation of rare artwork all bought admittance to the upper echelon, but even then, she was a step removed as a mere representative of the donor. She might be wealthy in her own right, but she'd worked hard to build her small fortune and it didn't come with the cachet of being born in the right family or having top two percent level money. Someday, someone would see through her facade and toss her out.

Neal held open the car door and she stepped into the Suburban. She didn't mind being driven around when she had work to do, and she was grateful not to have to split her attention between the road and the current issues facing the Mancuso family. She pulled a sheet of paper from her bag and pored over the contents of the document. Earlier in the day, she'd called one of her old clients, a hacker, and asked her to find out whatever she could about the car that had almost run her down. She'd been able to find out what their contact with the Dallas police had not. The company the car was registered to was a shell company and, based on her own research this afternoon, the owners could be traced back to the Petrov family holdings, ostensibly a real estate development company, but in real life a front for drugs and prostitution, two vices Carlo Mancuso refused to support.

A couple of months ago, Mikhail Petrov had approached Carlo with an offer to go into business together. Catering and event planning was a perfect front for the Petrovs' businesses, and the alliance seemed like a perfect fit until it became clear the Petrovs were more interested in gaining a screen for their prostitution ring than promoting their mutual efforts. Since Carlo abruptly cut ties with the Petrovs, little things had happened to undermine Mancuso family business, like the "anonymous" tip that led to the arrest of Jimmy G. But until the attempt on her life, which she was now convinced it was, there had been only nuisance happenings, nothing that warranted retaliatory action. But now that she'd confirmed Petrov was involved with the attempt on her life, Carlo was going to want to enact severe consequences for the Petrovs, a move that would escalate their acrimony, and which could prompt turf wars that would only distract from their day-to-day business. She skimmed the paper one more time, carefully folded it, and stuck it in the zipped pocket of her bag with the flash drive. Tomorrow. She'd share what she found with Carlo tomorrow, but tonight she would enjoy the illusion of attending a gala with a beautiful woman on her arm.

When Neal pulled up to the front of her apartment building, she told her not to park

"No problem." She pointed at the clock on the dashboard. "I'll wait down here."

"Take the night off. I've got it covered," she said.

Neal shook her head. "I promised I'd make sure you were accompanied."

She didn't have to ask who she'd promised. "Royal is picking me up tonight. I need to discuss some business with her," she said, immediately regretting giving in to the urge to explain. Since when did she feel the need to justify her actions to her employees? But Neal wasn't really her employee. Her loyalty was to the family in general and Carlo specifically. "Carlo asked me to talk to her. Besides, it's a gala at an art museum. I seriously doubt anyone is going to try to take me out in a room full of Picassos."

She stared at her for a moment and then shook her head. "Fine, but I'll be around. Call me if you need me."

"Always." She gathered her things and stepped out of the car. Knowing Neal, she wouldn't go far, keeping a subtle eye on her until she was back home for the night. She used to feel guilty at the constant attention to her safety, but she realized it was as much about protecting what she knew about the inner workings of the family empire as it was keeping her physically safe from harm. Neal's position in the organization was considered a privilege, and she got plenty of benefit from her close proximity to the inner circle without actually being in it. They were a lot alike that way.

Once she was in her apartment, she poured a finger of whiskey—enough to take the edge off, but not enough to impair her ability to perform. She stowed a notecard with her remarks in the tiny handbag she'd selected to go with her dress and stepped out of her lawyer drag and into a slim fitting burgundy cocktail dress. As she pulled the dress up her body, she remembered a different dress—the one she'd worn to Celia's wedding—and the model at Francine's who'd helped her dress and undress. She hadn't indulged since that day and she was starting to feel the jangling sensation she got when she was too wound up. Maybe, after the gala, she would detour to one of the bars she favored and remedy her restlessness with an attractive diversion.

Except she wouldn't be at the gala alone tonight, and the idea of dumping Royal in favor of some anonymous rendezvous felt distasteful. A new feeling for sure. She shoved away the thoughts and focused on getting ready. She'd just finished touching up her makeup and stepped into her new favorite Louboutins when the doorbell chimed. She downed the last drops of the whiskey and answered the door.

Royal was even more delicious than she had been at the wedding. She wore a tux like it was a second skin, seemingly unfazed by the formality of the outfit. What kind of woman went from jeans and boots to black tie with such ease, and where had she been all her life?

She handed her a bouquet of flowers. "You may want to put these in some water."

Realizing she'd been standing and staring, Siobhan held the door open wider. "Yes, of course. Please come in. Would you like a drink? We have a few minutes before we have to leave."

"Yes, thanks, that would be great."

Royal followed her to the kitchen, and Siobhan couldn't remember the last time she'd felt so self-conscious. Part of the issue was she never had anyone else in her home. Not anyone besides the family or Neal and her team anyway. The other part was wondering if Royal was sizing her up from behind. She knew she was attractive—it was one of the reasons she was able to get away with many things inside and outside of the courtroom—but she normally didn't care about the attribute except as a means to an end. Right now, she found herself hoping Royal appreciated the hours she spent at the gym and the way her dress hugged her curves, and the realization was both embarrassing and titillating.

"You have a beautiful home."

"Thank you." Siobhan looked around and appraised her surroundings. "I have everything I need here and it's comfortable." She turned her attention back to the bouquet, which was an unusual mix of purple chrysanthemums, eucalyptus, dusty miller, and succulents. "This is gorgeous. I don't think I've ever seen anything like it."

"Robert recommended the florist, but I picked out the arrangement. I'm not big on the standards."

"Noted." Siobhan reached for the bottle of Jameson Bow Street sitting on the sideboard. "Whiskey okay?"

"Whiskey is perfect." Royal smiled that rakish grin Siobhan was becoming very fond of and reached for the bottle. "And you have great taste."

"I promise I'm not trying to impress you because you know all things about spirits." She handed Royal a thick heavy glass. "I like what I like."

"To be liked by you is a compliment indeed."

Siobhan felt the warm creep of a blush on her neck. Time to turn this conversation in a different direction before she became completely distracted. "Have you been to the Dallas Museum of Art before?"

"No. I haven't been in town long enough to start exploring. What's it like?"

"The building itself is modern, but they have several very valuable and diverse collections and they do incorporate new finds as well. It's not New York or Paris level, but they're usually on the cutting edge of acquisitions." She wanted to ask Royal if she'd been to New York or Paris, and if she even enjoyed art museums at all or if she was only accompanying her tonight because she felt like she had to. But she kept quiet, partly because she didn't want to know if her answer was the latter. "I can't promise tonight won't be boring, but I will promise that I owe you one afterward."

Royal raised an eyebrow and grinned. "I doubt it will be boring, but I'm happy to have you in my debt." They sipped their whiskey in silence for a few moments, and then Royal placed the glass on the counter and crooked her arm. "Shall we go?"

Siobhan was a bit unsettled at how quickly Royal had settled into date mode, but she was even more unsettled at how much she liked it. She'd intended to suggest they take her car, but she kind of wanted Royal to be in charge. She pointed at the keys in Royal's hand. "Take me away."

❖

Royal handed the keys to the valet at the museum and rolled her eyes at the way he looked down his nose in disdain. The Jeep was part of the persona she played, but she actually liked it and didn't give a shit what this guy or anyone else thought about it. Surprisingly, Siobhan seemed not to mind what was likely a big downgrade on her usual mode of transport, and the ride over had consisted of idle conversation about the museum and the type of event they were in for this evening. With the Jeep in the hands of the valet, Royal placed her hand on Siobhan's elbow and guided her through the throng of people entering the museum and past the line of press hoping for a glimpse of someone famous entering the gala.

Siobhan moved through the crowd, giving only a slight nod to the reporters who called out her name. When they were inside, Royal took her coat and checked it along with hers. When she returned to Siobhan's side, she noticed she was holding two glasses of champagne. Royal took the one offered her way. "Look at you. I was barely gone a moment. I suppose being a celebrity has its perks."

Siobhan took a sip from her glass. "No celebrity here. Only money. Lots of it, and hardly any of it is mine. I'm merely a stand-in tonight." She motioned toward the door where the press waited for other notables to arrive. "They'll take photos of everyone who arrives and sort out who's who later. When they do, I doubt I'll make the cut."

Royal took note of the edge in her voice. It wasn't jealousy—more like sadness, but she couldn't quite place the emotion, so she pressed the point. "They knew your name."

Siobhan sighed. "It's unique."

"Family name?"

"It was my grandmother's."

"Ah. Are you close?"

"I never met her. I believe she's dead."

Siobhan delivered the statement as matter-of-factly as if she were reading the ingredients on a box of crackers. Royal searched her face, but other than a brief flash of pain in her eyes, her expression was steel. She remembered from Siobhan's file at the bureau that her mother had been estranged from the rest of the family, presumably because she'd had a child out of wedlock, but it was all supposition. She wanted to ask questions, but this wasn't the time. Instead, she reached for her hand, but Siobhan dodged the gesture and resumed the conversation as if it hadn't taken a dark detour.

"I'm often at these events as the family's representative," she said, "so the press is used to seeing me. That doesn't change the fact I'm not a Mancuso. They would go nuts if Dominique or Celia showed up here."

"And probably implode if Carlo arrived on scene," Royal said, watching carefully for Siobhan's reaction.

"He hates crowds, but he loves the art. His collection rivals some of the very best museums in the country, and he regularly loans pieces for exhibition because he truly believes the work of the masters is a gift to be shared." She grinned. "There was a time he would wear a hat and sunglasses and venture down here to visit exhibits anonymously. He loves to see the installations, and while many people would be focused on who I saw tonight and gossip about the other donors, I'll be tasked with reporting exactly how the pieces were displayed. Sometimes, I think he missed his calling as curator."

Royal smiled along with Siobhan, pleased she seemed to be comfortable sharing intimate details about Carlo so easily. She wanted to ask questions, find out more, but she didn't want to burst this bubble by pressing too hard, so she steered the subject in a new direction. "Do you enjoy the art or are you merely here out of duty?"

"Good question." Siobhan gazed at the walls in the room. "Why don't you answer that for yourself when the evening is over?"

Royal nodded, intrigued by her assignment. A waiter approached them with a tray of hors d'oeuvres. Siobhan smiled at the waiter and listened carefully as he described the morsel, both the ingredients and how it was made, with a patience none of the other patrons displayed. When he was done talking, she took the bite, placed it in her mouth, and moaned her approval.

"Royal, these are amazing. You must have one."

Royal dutifully complied, unable to resist Siobhan's eagerness. The tang of the bite hit her tongue and she moaned too. "This is amazing."

"Right?" Siobhan took another and thanked the waiter who moved on to the next group of guests. "The food here is always spot-on. Keep an eye out for the lobster wontons They'll go fast."

Royal grinned.

"What?" Siobhan asked, the second bit midway to her mouth.

"I guess I'm just surprised to see the badass lawyer and counselor to the don can be brought to her knees with a tiny bit of an appetizer."

"Small things are often underrated," Siobhan said. "Besides, food is a simple pleasure, but it's a balm for the soul, as my mother used to say. I may deny myself many things, but a delicious bite is not one of them."

Royal heard the hum of satisfaction in Siobhan's voice, but she couldn't tell if it was directed at her. She wanted it to be, though, and that was a problem. Time to refocus on the reason she was here in the first place. "Besides delicious food, what else happens at these things?"

"'These things' consist of a lot of preening on the part

of the museum staff, several boring speeches, and a pressure campaign to give more money."

"I was hoping we'd get a private tour."

"I'm sure that can be arranged. I'm one of the speechmakers, but after I'm done, I'll show you around."

"I look forward to it." And just like that, they were back to flirting, and Royal surrendered to it. She needed to make headway on this case so she could be done with it, and if flirting with a beautiful, accomplished, and complicated woman was the way to get there, she was all in. Amazingly, it came fairly easy considering it had been a long time since she'd had the opportunity. She'd been on her last case for six months, deep in the belly of the Garza organization, handling logistics for their drug running operation over the border. She'd been one of the few women working for the cartel, and the vapid women who hung around the fringe with their singular focus on drugs and partying weren't her type. Not that she was averse to having fun. She simply liked her recreation with a little more depth for when the party died down. If she couldn't have a meaningful conversation with a woman, she may as well satisfy her physical needs by her own hand or with a hooker and save herself from having to endure the small talk.

"Siobhan, you came."

A tall, handsome man with dark, wavy hair appeared at Siobhan's side and pulled her into a hug. Royal immediately sensed Siobhan freeze up at the approach and her own senses went on high alert.

"Hello, Martin. I didn't expect to see you here," Siobhan said, her friendly tone covering for the displeasure conveyed by the way she barely offered her hand and sidestepped his embrace.

"Dad insisted. He couldn't be here, and he wanted to make sure the family was represented." He looked around. "I haven't seen Carlo, so I'm assuming you're here for the same reason."

Royal watched Siobhan's brow crease and knew that on some level the assumption everyone made that Siobhan was just another Mancuso daughter weighed heavy. She had the authority, the power, but when it came down to ride or die loyalty, would the family stand with her, no matter what? Royal filed the thought away in the box labeled "ways to turn Siobhan Collins" and directed her attention at Mr. Handsome who was practically drooling over her date. She stuck out her hand. "Hi, I'm Royal Flynn."

He squeezed her hand with a firm grip. "Martin Vedda." He glanced back and forth between them. "How do you two know each other?"

"Business." Both of them uttered the word at the same time. Royal caught Siobhan's eye and grinned. Siobhan really was captivating and, bonus, she didn't seem to realize it. What had it been like to grow up in the shadow of Dominique and Celia Mancuso? Whatever it had been, Siobhan had more than survived. According to the file she'd read, she'd been top of her class and editor of the law review, and then she'd gone into business for herself within a week of passing the bar. Sure, she'd probably had help from Carlo to be able to attend in the first place, but money only went so far. Siobhan had clearly worked her butt off at school and demonstrated a passion for a good fight. That she would be able to use those talents as part of her work was a bonus, but her expertise would count against her once she was arrested and charged for every single time she crossed the line. She'd be unable to claim she didn't know what the Mancuso family was really up to behind the scenes of their community ties and philanthropy. Royal knew she should relish the idea of Siobhan and the rest of the Mancuso operation behind bars, but in this moment, the only image she wanted to enjoy was Siobhan in her form-fitting dress standing beside her.

Clearly, it had been too long since she'd had a normal life. Royal tried to recall the last time she'd been on a real date. It had been way longer than the time she'd worked on the Garza case. It might have been a few years. Yep, it had been Maria, the cousin of one of the other agents in her division. She'd gone in with high hopes because Maria, unlike other women she'd dated in the past, had known from the start that she was an agent who often worked undercover, and it had started well. They'd enjoyed dinner and drinks, and conversation about likes and dislikes late into the night. A second date had delivered more of the same, but when the conversation led to deeper topics, like family and work, Royal ran into her usual problem, unable to share personal details with someone she barely knew. She couldn't talk specific details about her work, and as for her family, she wasn't interested in rehashing the trouble she'd managed to escape, and Ryan? She never knew what to say about her little brother. When he'd joined the military, she'd had high hopes he'd find his way, figure out how to get his life on track, but his sudden return home left her wondering if he ever would.

"Have you given any more thought to my ideas?"

Royal tuned back into the conversation in time to hear Martin's question, directed at Siobhan. Siobhan's drawn brow suggested she was annoyed at the query, or maybe she was more annoyed at the fact he'd chosen to bring up business at a gala. Whatever the case, Royal listened closely while trying to maintain an appearance of nonchalance.

"I'm looking into it," Siobhan said.

"Time is of the essence."

"Everyone says that," she replied. "What that usually

means is that the person asking for the dispensation is impatient, which is not a good sign."

Martin merely smiled in response to the shade. "It's hard to be patient about a sure thing. You're too cautious." He laughed and leaned closer to Siobhan, his voice dripping with a mix of familiarity and condescension. "You always were. It would do you good to let loose a little."

Royal wanted to growl at him for his sexist remarks. He wouldn't talk this way to another man, but it wasn't her place to defend Siobhan's honor—it would only reinforce the image of her as a weak woman who didn't know how to handle real business. She could, however, respond to his attempt to act like he and Siobhan had some special bond. She placed her hand on Siobhan's arm. "I thought this was a gala. Shall we go find another drink and have a little fun?" she asked, keeping her voice light and flirty.

Martin's eyes narrowed like he was trying to figure out the layers of their relationship and expecting Siobhan to turn Royal down in favor of staying in his presence. Royal doubted there was much he wanted he couldn't have, but Siobhan would surely make that list.

Siobhan laced her fingers through Royal's. "You're absolutely right. Let's find that drink." She gave Martin a small wave as they walked away. "Don't worry. You'll hear from me. One way or another."

They'd barely reached the bar when a man at the front of the room tapped his finger on the microphone and called Siobhan's name. "Looks like you're on," Royal said.

Siobhan barely hid a slight grimace. "Looks like. Wait for me?"

"Of course. Don't think I've forgotten about my private tour. Go be the face of the Mancuso family, but when you're done, I'm claiming you for the rest of the night." She watched Siobhan's face for her reaction to the bold statement and was pleasantly surprised when the initial reaction was a broad smile.

"'Claiming,' you say? Interesting." Siobhan released her hand slowly, like she was contemplating choosing to stay instead of giving her speech. When their grasp slipped, she leaned close to Royal's ear. "We'll see who will be claiming who. Just you wait."

She turned and walked away before Royal could react. Damn, it was getting hard to focus.

Siobhan was almost to the stage when Royal felt her phone buzz in her pocket. It was the "official" phone she'd been issued for this case, and the only people who had the number were Wharton, Robert, and Siobhan. Of course, Robert could've given the number to anyone, but she pulled it out with a sense of dread to see Wharton's private number on the screen. In all the time she'd been working undercover, he had never called her burner phone, choosing some other, less obvious way to reach out. He would only call if it was an emergency, but if she were to duck out now, it would definitely be noticed. The phone continued to buzz as the emcee urged everyone to turn their attention to Siobhan. She considered turning it off, but her instincts told her to answer. She glanced to the left and spotted an alcove. She edged her way out of the throng of people, but by the time she was secluded in the semi-private space, the phone had stopped ringing. She started to push redial, but the incoming text paralyzed her. The words were simple and terrifying.

BOMB THREAT. GET OUT NOW!

CHAPTER ELEVEN

Siobhan stood at the podium, staring out at all the expectant faces, wishing once again Carlo hadn't stopped attending these events. When she was younger, he would escort her into the room, introduce her around to the socialite crowd, and ask her to wait while he made a few remarks. The crowd would politely clap in response, and then he would rejoin her for a private tour with the curator, who showed them some of the new acquisitions, as befitted a generous megadonor. On many such occasions, a docent would refer to her as Carlo's daughter, a mistake she would quickly correct, often wondering if she hadn't taken the step, what would Carlo have said. Last year, he'd turned the duty of making a speech over to her, but at least he'd still accompanied her for the occasion. Carlo might not be part of Dallas society's in-crowd, but people respected him even if it was a respect laced with fear, and they'd always treated her well. But here by herself for the first time, she suspected most of these people were a bit disdainful at her lack of pedigree and the fact she was only a representative of the actual donor.

Thank God for Royal's presence tonight. She settled her gaze on Royal, who stood in the back of the room, casually leaning against the wall with a drink in her hand. She flashed a slow smile, as if transmitting a relaxed vibe all the way across the room. They might barely know each other, but Siobhan was infused with confidence simply by being in Royal's strong, calm presence. She took a deep breath and spoke into the microphone. "On behalf of the entire Mancuso family, I would like to extend my thanks to the museum board and all of the volunteers who make it possible to share the works of many famous and soon to be famous artists from around the world with the citizens of Dallas."

She droned on a bit, or that's how it sounded in her head, rattling off statistics about the effect of art on society and conveying praise for how this museum was bringing some of the finest acquisitions to the city. She was near the end of the remarks she'd prepared when she noticed Royal pull her phone out of her pocket and stare at the screen. Royal's eyes widened and she flashed a quick look toward the podium before ducking out of the room. Siobhan had no idea what she said after that, consumed with curiosity about what had urgently diverted Royal's attention in another direction.

"The Mancuso family thanks the museum for this honor, and in conclusion, I'd like to offer my congratulations—"

A loud siren rang through the air, drowning out the rest of the sentence. "What the hell was that?" Siobhan said, neglecting to remember she was still holding the microphone. Uniformed men burst through the back door and began fanning out into the crowd. At first Siobhan thought they were museum security, but then she recognized the familiar uniforms of the Dallas Police Department. She slid the button to turn off the mic and dropped it onto the podium.

"Please," one of the officers called out to the crowd. "Everyone remain calm. We need you to exit the building in an orderly fashion."

His words were like a referee's starting whistle, and

the throng of people who moments ago had been lounging around, tossing back drinks, eating passed canapés, and one-upping each other about the size of their donations were now a stampede of cattle, determined to break the fence and run to freedom.

More cops poured into the room in an attempt to quell the action. The one that had been coming toward her yelled even louder, "Come on. All of you need to go."

She started to retort, something along the lines of they didn't have any business ordering her around, but she barely had her mouth open to reply when she was startled by a strong arm circling her waist, and a whispered voice in her ear. "This way."

She let Royal lead her around the edge of the crowd, noting the irony of refusing to leave when the cops ordered her to do, but not hesitating to follow Royal to God knows where. "What's going on?"

"The police think there's a bomb in the building and they've ordered an evacuation."

She held back a gasp and forced her voice to calm. "You think they could've just said so."

"I'm sure they were trying to keep the crowd under control. You saw how everyone reacted when they asked people to leave."

Royal's assured confidence that had been attractive a moment ago suddenly seemed a little suspect. "And how do you know what the police think?"

Royal blinked, the movement so subtle most people wouldn't have noticed, but Siobhan was skilled in the art of reading nonverbal cues from witnesses and juries, and she applied her expertise here. "Tell me what's going on."

"I heard them talking." Royal gestured to the back of the room where she'd been standing moments ago. "I stepped outside to see what was going on and heard the word *bomb*. They're not a subtle bunch. While they were huddled around, trying to figure out what to do, I asked one of the docents for the closest exit behind the podium and she gave me directions. I figure everyone else will be heading out the front doors and we can slip away in the back. It's not like the valet is going to be sending runners into the parking garage to get cars if there's a bomb on site." She stopped and pointed. "Here, it's through there."

Siobhan pushed on the exit door and winced as the clang of the alarm blended with the warning siren already blaring throughout the entire museum. Royal pointed to the right and they stepped out into the cool night air. Siobhan pulled out her phone. "I should try to reach the director on the phone and see if they're planning to try to resume once the police have searched the building."

Royal shook her head. "Don't count on it. They'll spend hours checking every space in the building, and there are a lot of places someone could hide an explosive device."

There was something both assured and unsettling about her cool demeanor under the circumstance, and it piqued Siobhan's curiosity. "You sound like you know a bit about bombings," Siobhan said, lobbing the remark into the conversation to see Royal's reaction.

"I do. I was an explosives specialist in the Army. Two tours in Afghanistan. It feels like a lifetime ago, but some things you never forget."

Siobhan nodded, wondering how a former specialist in the Army had wound up selling booze for a living. No wonder Royal was up for more action. She filed the information away to be more fully examined at a later time. She reached into her purse. "I'll call Neal. She'll come pick us up."

Royal held up her phone. "I've got an Uber coming.

They'll be here in about three minutes." She glanced back at the door and took Siobhan's arm. "Look, I know you'd probably prefer the protection you're used to, but I assure you, I'm perfectly capable of taking care of you."

The words were delivered in a soft, silky tone, and Siobhan let herself fall under Royal's spell, not minding at all the fact she was surrendering control. "Fine. Besides, I imagine if we hang around here much longer, the press will find us, and I'd rather not have to comment on something when I have no idea what's happening. I'll call Neal from the car. We have contacts at the police department who might be able to let us know what's going on."

A large, midnight blue Yukon pulled into the parking lot and headed their way. Royal confirmed it was their ride and led them toward the passenger side of the SUV. Siobhan let Royal help her make the step into the vehicle and then proceeded to send a string of texts to Neal before putting away her phone in time to hear Royal tell the driver they'd be making two stops. The idea of cutting short their evening left her feeling bereft. She placed a hand on Royal's arm and addressed the driver directly. "Strike that." She gave her address, and before she could change her mind, she met Royal's questioning look and said, "I want a stiff drink. Care to join me?"

Royal studied her for a moment and Siobhan tried not to flinch under the penetrating gaze. No one had ever made her feel so off balance, and she'd certainly never imagined she would enjoy the sensation as much as she did.

"I would absolutely love to join you," Royal said, finally.

Siobhan nodded slowly, wanting to acknowledge the response, but fearing if she spoke her voice might tremble with anticipatory desire. Royal was coming home with her, and she might need more than a stiff drink to cap off the evening.

❖

Royal was desperate to check her phone again, but there was no chance she could sneak a look as Siobhan was sitting less than an inch away in the back of the Uber. Besides, she'd find out whatever she needed to know from Wharton later. Her curiosity didn't warrant arousing suspicion now, not when Siobhan seemed to have let down her guard. Within fifteen minutes of leaving the museum, they pulled up to Siobhan's apartment building.

"Pull up to the valet stand," Siobhan told the driver. "They won't mind."

When the car pulled to a halt, Royal jumped out on her side and walked briskly around the back of the vehicle to open Siobhan's door. She held her arm as she stepped out, and she couldn't help but notice Siobhan's well-toned leg sliding past her as she stepped down onto the pavement. She spoke to keep from staring. "Are you sure you want me to come up?"

Siobhan stared at her for a moment, her expression unreadable. "No, but I want you to anyway. Follow me." Siobhan strode through the lobby to a bank of elevators. Once inside, she inserted her keycard in the slot and pushed the button for the penthouse. The elevator shot up, and Royal watched the numbers fly by as they passed all of the numbered floors.

"You look uncomfortable. Do you not like heights?" Siobhan asked, wearing a playful grin.

"I'm not a huge fan, but I can handle anything."

"Is that so?" Siobhan stepped closer. "That is a very all-encompassing statement. 'Anything'? Really?"

"What doesn't kill you makes you stronger. Or so I've

heard." Royal leaned back against the rear wall of the elevator car. "I'm guessing you like heights very much."

"I'm not a big fan either, but these buildings rarely put the nicest suites on the bottom floors, so I've learned to make do."

Royal stepped closer. "And you like nice things."

"I do." Siobhan's breath hitched. "Is there something wrong with that?"

"Not at all." She lifted her hand and lightly stroked the hair behind Siobhan's left ear. It was as soft and silky as she'd imagined, and the dark strands fanned out across her fingers like silken feathers.

Siobhan ran her hand down Royal's arm until she reached her hand. She laced her fingers through Royal's and lifted their connected hands to eye level. "See this? This is a nice thing."

The doors opened just then, revealing several tourist types who looked like they were late for dinner. Royal gazed at them with dread, but Siobhan grabbed her hand and tugged. "Let's get off here."

Royal dutifully complied and followed Siobhan a few steps away to a different elevator bank. "How many elevators does this place have?"

"Not enough, apparently," Siobhan replied, punching the elevator call button repeatedly. When the car finally came, they rode the one floor up in silence. When they reached her apartment door, Siobhan pulled out a key and turned it in the lock. She took a step inside and looked over her shoulder. "Are you coming in?"

Royal followed her through the door and clasped her hand deciding she may as well go big or go home. Siobhan didn't clasp back, but she didn't let go either, simply leading the way inside. Siobhan gently released her hand and strolled into the living room toward an enormous bar full of wood and glass and elegant bottles. She reached for the bottle of Jameson Bow Street. "I assume you're good to keep drinking whiskey?"

"If you keep pouring me that, I'm going to be spoiled for life."

Siobhan held it up. "It is a nice bottle."

"It's what's in it that makes the difference. The whiskey is aged for eighteen years and it's only bottled once a year."

"I'm very familiar. And you're right, it's become very popular lately, but I've always liked it." Siobhan poured three fingers in a chunky glass and handed it her way. "I'm glad you like it too."

Royal wanted to wax poetic about how very much she liked the whiskey, but she remembered the person she was playing might sell fine booze, but that didn't mean she had the means to stash much away for herself. "I like it very much, but it's not exactly in my budget."

"All the more reason to drink my stash." Siobhan poured a glass for herself and tilted it her way. "Cheers to being able to afford good whiskey and cheers to near misses."

It took Royal a minute to realize she was referring to the bomb threat at the museum. She clinked her glass against Siobhan's and took a deep drink. "I wonder what happened."

"I'm sure we'll find out soon. Especially if it made it onto the news." As if on cue, Siobhan's purse started vibrating. She fished it from her bag and stared at the screen.

"Everything okay?" Royal asked, wishing she felt comfortable enough to check her own phone.

Siobhan held up the screen so Royal could see the cascade of messages. "Carlo might be a tad worried. I need to make a call. Make yourself at home. I'll be right back."

Royal watched her go, relieved to be left alone to explore but curious about what was up. Likely Carlo had seen the news about the bomb scare and was worried about his consigliere.

She took advantage of Siobhan's absence to check her own phone, but all she had was a vague text from Wharton that essentially said he'd fill her in later. She considered trying to listen at the door Siobhan had just shut behind her, but it would be hard to explain if she was caught. A better use of her time would be to see what else of interest she could find in Siobhan's apartment, and she had a lot of ground to cover, starting with the tiny handbag Siobhan had left on the counter. Searching the bag took all of two seconds. The entire contents consisted of a tube of lipstick, a compact, and a thin wallet with her license and a black American Express card. The card might be helpful since cardholders had to spend an exorbitant amount a year to have one. Judging by the looks of this place, Siobhan certainly indulged in a lot of creature comforts, but she might also be running purchases for the family business through her personal account. Royal took a quick picture of the credit card and moved on to the desk on the other side of the room. She pulled out the drawer and carefully thumbed through the contents. Stamps, a random assortment of envelopes, and a few paperclips, but nothing of note. She pushed the drawer shut and looked around.

The oversized living room was exceptionally well decorated, but short on hiding places. Royal casually walked through the room to give the appearance she was merely killing time, but she studied every inch of the space just in case. When she reached the far corner where the fireplace was located, she noticed a basket, about the size of a footstool, tucked away in the corner. She stepped closer and stared at the outside. It looked old. An antique maybe? Antique or not, it stood out in stark contrast to the more modern feel of the rest of the room. She reached for the lid and carefully lifted the edge.

"It was my mother's."

Shit. Royal took a breath and slowly turned around.

Siobhan was standing across the room, her dark eyes furrowed, her hands on her hips. "It's like one my mother had," Royal lied. She pointed at the basket. "She kept all her sewing notions in it." She smiled. "We were never allowed to touch anything inside. Was your mom the same way?"

Siobhan stared a moment longer before her expression finally relaxed. "She was. But her basket was for stationery and pens. She wrote down all her new recipes by hand. And she used to send handwritten letters. I always thought she was very old-fashioned, but here I am, hanging on to her things many years later like they're some kind of treasure."

Royal walked to Siobhan's side, praying she was reading Siobhan's mood correctly. She reached for her hand. "Memories are a treasure. The very best kind. They're priceless and no one can take them away from you." She lobbed the comment out as bait, sensing if she knew more about Siobhan's childhood, she might root out the reason for Siobhan's loyalty to a family that wasn't her own.

Siobhan turned toward her, her face only inches away. Royal stayed still under her penetrating gaze, waiting patiently, suddenly very aware she was no longer interested in conversation. She knew what she wanted to happen next, but Siobhan would need to make the first move.

She didn't have to wait long. Siobhan leaned closer and pressed her lips against Royal's. Softly at first. Gentle velvet kisses growing slowly in intensity. By the time Siobhan slid her tongue between her lips, Royal felt she would come undone. She couldn't remember the last time she'd felt this aroused and she wanted nothing more than to surrender to it. She groaned as Siobhan's touch became more intense, and she placed a hand on either side of Siobhan's waist and drew her closer.

Siobhan took the cue and she tugged at Royal's shirt until

it was hanging from her waistband. She ran her fingers up the length of Royal's back, lightly dragging her nails along her flesh, leaving a trail of desire in the wake of her steamy touch. Royal placed a hand on the mantel of the fireplace to brace against the way her body was bowing to Siobhan's touch, but the control was only temporary. She was a master when it came to playing a role, but in this moment, she wasn't playing. If she didn't get Siobhan naked, in bed, soon, she would lose her mind.

CHAPTER TWELVE

Siobhan reluctantly released the kiss and took Royal's hand. She was breaking all her rules—no women at her house, no sex with anyone on the family payroll—but after Carlo's report that the police had indeed found a bomb at the museum tonight, she wasn't in a rule-abiding mood. All she could think about was getting Royal out of her tux and into her bed. Now.

She led the way to her bedroom, determined to assume control and wishing she could surrender all of it at the same time. When they crossed the threshold, she pointed to the bed. "I'll be right back."

When she was alone in the bathroom, she slipped out of her dress and into a scarlet silk negligee. She stared at her reflection in the mirror. Her hair was mussed from Royal's hands and her lips were swollen from their extended kissing session. Her reflection screamed vulnerability, and while her every instinct told her to hide any weakness, she shoved those feelings away and resolved to surrender to desire.

The room was dark when she reentered, except for the flicker of candlelight from her nightstand. Royal was propped against the pillows, and the shadows danced across her completely naked body. She looked confident, comfortable, and completely at ease. The combination was a heady intoxicant Siobhan couldn't resist.

"I hope you don't mind that I lit the candle," Royal said, her voice low and husky.

Siobhan traced a finger along her leg. "Looks like you did a bit more than that. And no, I don't mind at all." She reached down and lightly kissed the inside of her thigh, enjoying the way Royal moaned at the slightest touch. "You're very expressive for someone with such a tough exterior."

Royal reached for her hand and kissed her palm, sending shock waves through her entire body. Her eyes fluttered shut and she didn't even try to hold back a growl of pleasure.

"I could say the same about you," Royal said, her lips curled in a self-satisfied smile.

Siobhan climbed into the bed and hovered above Royal's body, dipping to run her tongue along Royal's neck. "Perhaps you bring something out in me."

"You mean you're usually not a tigress in bed?"

Siobhan laughed. "I don't know about that, but I'm usually not someone who invites women back to my own bed." She waved a hand to indicate the room. "This is my sanctuary."

"What's different?"

Siobhan considered not answering since she'd already shared more than she'd planned, but something about Royal made her want to open up. Hell, Royal was naked in her bed and she'd just admitted inviting her here was out of character. She seemed to have no power to resist Royal's curiosity. Or she didn't want to. She ignored the voice inside telling her to be more circumspect and plunged ahead. "Maybe it's because we had a brush with death. Maybe I simply feel comfortable with you." She paused. "Or both."

Royal reached up and placed a hand on her cheek. "Whatever the reason, I'm grateful to be here."

Her voice was tender and sweet, and Siobhan wanted to respond in kind, but a lifetime of guarding her feelings held her back. Wasn't it enough she'd invited Royal to stay? Did she have to lower her inhibitions entirely? She could have fun without sacrificing control. She rolled over on her side and pulled Royal with her until their positions were reversed. "No need to be grateful, but I do need you to fuck me. Are you interested?"

A brief flash of emotion flashed in Royal's eyes—pain, regret? She couldn't tell and she shouldn't care, but she did, and she chose to hide it behind a casual posture while she waited an eternity for Royal to respond.

"Sure, I'm always down for a good fuck."

Siobhan nearly flinched at the sting of the rough remark, but she was determined not to surrender to her feelings because if she did, she'd be consumed with Royal's tender kisses, her protective nature, her easy smile. From the moment Royal had pushed her out of the path of the SUV to the moment she'd shown up at the Mancuso mansion, Siobhan had been taken with her confidence, her good looks, and her charm. The very fact Royal was here right now was a testament to the depth of the attraction and how very dangerous it might be. If she truly wanted to avoid this pitfall, she'd ask Royal to leave before this—whatever this was—went any further.

But Royal was naked and stretched out over the length of her, the proximity of their bodies nearly setting her skin on fire. When Royal ran a finger along the inside of her thigh, her body rose to meet the touch, unaware her mind was doing battle with her emotions and her mind was losing the fight. *Pretend she's the model from the dress shop or the bartender from the speakeasy you visited the week before. Imagine these hands, these glorious, gentle, skillful hands belong to a woman whose name you do not know and that you will never meet again. You can do this. All you have to do is pretend you're somewhere other than here and Royal is a stranger who'll be gone before dawn.*

She closed her eyes and arched to meet Royal's touch again. She vowed this would be the only time she'd give in to her craving for this woman, but right now, in this moment, she surrendered to the dancing flames of arousal and pretended she and Royal were more than they would ever be in real life.

❖

Royal slipped her hands underneath Siobhan's body and pulled her closer, savoring the taste of her. With each pass of her tongue, Siobhan groaned and arched closer, sure signs she was enjoying herself, but her eyes remained closed and Royal realized Siobhan wasn't truly present, and she could be anyone as long as she kept up the steady pressure on the path to Siobhan's organism.

The question was why did she care? This was a job. Okay, being naked with Siobhan was a seriously good benefit of the job, but it meant nothing. She'd had sex with strangers while on the job before, all part of playing a role, doing whatever was necessary to gather intel, garner trust, get the job done. She'd even felt affection for her marks before, sometimes regretting her lack of feeling about the act, especially when it was clear the balance of feelings was weighted against her. But this was different because this time she was the one with feelings while Siobhan was merely going through the motions.

Or was she? Siobhan had made the first move. And the second. They wouldn't be in her bed right now if it wasn't what she wanted. Royal had been certain she'd detected more than chemistry between them. Had the deeper attraction been one-sided? She told herself she only cared because of the case.

The more Siobhan liked her and trusted her, the more likely she'd be able to get close enough to wedge her way into the Mancuso inner circle.

She looked up at Siobhan's still closed eyes, and Royal was suddenly determined to shake her back to the present. She flattened her tongue and slowly drew it along Siobhan's clit as she slid first one then two fingers into the heat of her sex. Siobhan thrashed on the bed in response to the touch, but Royal didn't relent. She murmured, "Do you want me to stop?"

"No. Please don't."

Pleased she'd been able to elicit a verbal response, Royal answered with a long, slow, swipe of her tongue down the side of Siobhan's clit, burrowing into the heat, determined to bring her to climax. Everything else in the world fell away as Siobhan cried out and stiffened against her unrelenting touch. She had no idea how much time had passed when Siobhan thrashed with her building orgasm, but she kept her lips pressed against her sex, savoring the smell and taste of her.

When Siobhan finally stopped trembling, Royal eased out from between her legs and moved back up to the headboard to lie beside her. She wanted to curl up against Siobhan and spend the balance of the night in this cocoon, but she was careful not to slip into the familiarity of a lover. She lay on her back with her hands behind her head and breathed deep, in and out, to quell her own arousal while she wondered how long it would take for Siobhan to suggest it was time for her to go. A few minutes passed with them lying there in silence, and Royal decided it would be better to initiate her own exit. She leaned over and kissed Siobhan on the cheek. "You are amazing. Thanks for letting me burn off the adrenaline, but I should get going. At some point, they're going to have to let people get their cars."

Siobhan stared, her brow furrowed as if trying to decide

what to say, but Royal didn't give her a chance. She rolled out of bed and started collecting her clothes from the floor.

"Thanks for going with me tonight," Siobhan said, finally breaking the silence. "I promise these events are usually very boring and very rarely involve bomb squads and secret Uber escapes."

Royal forced a grin. "So you say. I suppose I'll just have this one to judge." She let the comment hang in the air, expecting Siobhan to say something along the lines of "no, there'll be other times," but Siobhan's lack of a response left her wondering what tonight had been all about. Siobhan had a reputation for assignations, and she'd played on that, but now it seemed Siobhan was done playing. Royal had been confident she could get Siobhan to warm up to her, but maybe she'd moved too fast, too soon, and now she fell into the category of one-night stands never to be repeated. If this were real life, she wouldn't care, having never bothered to develop a relationship with another woman since doing so was like crossing a field scattered with landmines made up of all the lies she'd had to tell about her work. But this wasn't real life. She had a role to play and an investigation to pursue, and she wasn't going to be successful if she couldn't convince Siobhan she was different from all the other women who traipsed through her bedroom.

She fastened the buttons on her shirt and tossed her jacket over her arm. Siobhan was propped up in bed, her dark hair fanned out on the silk pillowcases. She strode over and ran the back of her hand along the dark tresses. "So soft." She leaned down and captured Siobhan's lips in a kiss, careful to keep it from deepening and pulling away when Siobhan pressed in. "Thank you for inviting me. It was the perfect first date."

She straightened up and plastered on a broad smile. She could tell by Siobhan's confused expression that she wasn't sure whether she was kidding about the date remark, which was exactly the reaction she wanted. She blew a kiss. "I'll see myself out. Sweet dreams."

She strode to the bedroom door with mixed feelings about the fact Siobhan had snuggled down into the covers, apparently taking her up on her offer. Royal closed the bedroom door behind her and took the hallway back to the living room. Had it been the wrong move to leave so abruptly? Should she have stayed the night to solidify whatever this was that was going on between them?

Lost in her thoughts, she almost didn't notice the briefcase sitting on the table in the foyer. Had it been there before? She hadn't had a chance to look here before Siobhan had surprised her in the living room as she was about to open her mother's antique basket.

She glanced over her shoulder. The silence in the apartment was thick, and she wondered if Siobhan had fallen asleep. If she was still in her room, it was about twenty good-sized steps from there to here. Five seconds give or take from the noise of footfalls to the loss of opportunity. Was the risk of being caught worth it?

She carefully unfastened the latch and pulled the briefcase open. It was practically empty save for a legal pad and a Visconti fountain pen. She stared at the zippered inside pocket and looked around the still silent room. She held her breath as she eased the zipper open and ran her fingers along the inside. A paper crinkled against her touch and she felt something small, hard with squared edges. She pulled it out and examined the flash drive. If she had the luxury of time, she could copy the contents onto her phone, but doing so with Siobhan only steps away was a risk too far.

She should put it back and try again later. But what if it was gone? It was Friday night, the weekend. She could surely put it back before Siobhan noticed it was missing. All she had to do was come up with some reason to come back here—it wasn't like she didn't want to anyway.

Decision made, she shoved the drive in her pocket and zipped the inside compartment of Siobhan's briefcase shut and fastened the bag shut. Moments later, she was in a car that wasn't hers, headed to the house she didn't own. The only thing that had been real about tonight was her unrelenting attraction to Siobhan, and the reality was she'd just betrayed her.

CHAPTER THIRTEEN

Siobhan rolled over in bed and reached for her phone on the nightstand. She scrunched her eyes at the screen, but getting them to focus was a monumental task. She reached into her nightstand for the readers she used when she had to sit up late reading legal briefs and slipped them on. *Shit.* It was eleven a.m. She'd never slept this late and, on top of that, she must've shut the ringer off—something she only ever did when she was in court—because a long line of missed calls greeted her. She swung out of bed, grabbed her silk robe from her closet, and made her way to the kitchen, where she started a large pot of coffee as fortification for the string of messages.

Carlo, his voice laced with concern: *"Patatino, check in with me as soon as you receive this message."*

Carlo again, with an undercurrent of frustration: *"Neal says she hasn't seen you yet this morning. You promised me last night you would come to the house for brunch, but no one has heard from you. Neal said she knocked on your door, but you haven't answered."*

Dominique, annoyed: *"Where are you? Poppa is worried and wants to know why you haven't called him back. I told him you were probably working to show how even a bomb threat doesn't throw you off track, but he's tasked me with making sure you're okay, so this is me doing my part. Brunch was great, by the way."*

Neal, concerned: *"I'm sure you know by now that everyone is looking for you. I know you haven't left your apartment, but someone else did. I respect your privacy as much as the next person, but if I don't hear from you in the next thirty minutes, I'm breaking down the door."*

Siobhan looked at the time of her call and realized she'd probably be planning her break-in in the next few minutes. She cinched the tie of her robe and made it to the door just as the loud pounding started. She swung the door wide. "Thank goodness I don't have any neighbors, or you would've woken them all up by now."

Neal's expression transformed from frantic to cautiously relaxed in a matter of seconds. She motioned to Pete, who was standing behind her, and told him to stay put before following Siobhan back into the apartment and shutting the door behind them. "What's with the communication blackout?"

"What's with the lack of respect for my privacy?" she snapped back, annoyed at the continued intrusion on her morning after. She walked to the kitchen and poured a cup of coffee, intentionally not offering one to her. "You knew I was in for the night, and obviously you've been watching, so you know I haven't left. Am I not allowed to have some time to myself?"

"But you weren't alone all night, were you?" She scowled. "You are aware that someone is trying to kill you, right? You bring a woman home, and she leaves and then it's radio silence from you. You ignored calls from Carlo, Dominique, and me, which is completely out of character. Who's to say you weren't lying here dead?"

"Wait, you thought…" Siobhan had trouble wrapping her mind around the idea Neal or anyone else in her family thought Royal was in her apartment doing her harm when Royal had done the exact opposite, right up until the moment she'd abruptly left. "Never mind. As you can see, I'm fine." She flicked her hand in Neal's direction. "You can go report back to whoever you need to that all is well."

She glanced over her shoulder, but she didn't move.

"What is it?" she asked.

"You're not going to like this."

Her stomach spun with dread. "Tell me."

"Last night wasn't just a threat. There *was* a bomb at the museum. The don doesn't want us to leave you alone. We're to stay with you, round-the-clock and close by."

Siobhan stared at her for a moment as she sorted through her words. She already knew from her conversation with Carlo last night the police had recovered a bomb. If it had gone off, a large portion of Dallas high society would've been caught in the blast and the event would've occupied headlines for days. She got that it was a big deal, but what did that have to do with a complete loss of privacy for her?

"He thinks you were the target. He thinks—"

"Wait." Siobhan held up her hand to get her to stop talking. She was already having trouble digesting his message, but the idea someone might have placed a bomb in a building packed with people for the sole purpose of targeting her was more than she could handle. She sagged against the counter, and within seconds, Neal was at her side, leading her to the living room. She settled onto the couch and motioned for her to sit in the chair across from her.

"Hang on, I'll be right back," she said before disappearing into the kitchen instead.

She stared after her, but she didn't have the energy to protest. The near miss from the SUV was one thing, but using a mass casualty incident to send a message to the Mancuso family was over the top. Mikhail Petrov was a vicious man, but was he stupid enough to risk the level of law enforcement scrutiny that would come from killing dozens of innocent people? She supposed it was possible, but she was skeptical despite the fact no other plausible explanation came to mind.

"Here, take this."

Neal handed her a glass of water, and when she took it from her, she held out her other hand, palm up. She stared at the small, white oval pill and shook her head. "You know I don't do drugs."

"It's prescription."

"Not mine."

"Seriously? It's the smallest dose, but it'll take the edge off."

She hesitated. She could use a horse tranquilizer right now, but she needed a clear mind more. "My edge is what makes me effective. Keep your pills for yourself, and don't ever let Don Carlo catch you with them. You'll be out in an instant." She stared while she shrugged and placed the pill in her pocket, hoping she understood "be out" was a permanent state of being. "I need you to be sharp. We're being attacked. If they would go after me like this, then the entire family is in danger."

"You think it's Petrov."

"What do you think?" she asked, genuinely curious about her opinion.

"It could be him. He knows you're valuable to the don, but because you're not a blood relation, he figures he can send a message by hurting you without risking an all-out war."

She shuddered. Neal was right. She wasn't family. Attacking her directly would send a message without incurring the hellfire wrath that killing one of Carlo's children would bring.

"I'm sorry," she said. "That was crass."

"It was honest, and honesty is exactly what I need right now." Neal's words stung, but she was right, and Siobhan had ignored the implications at her peril. "We have work to do."

"This means we'll be canceling the meeting with Petrov." Her conclusory tone indicated she thought it was a foregone conclusion.

"No."

"You're kidding, right? You really want to walk into a meeting with him when it's possible the man is set on killing you?"

She didn't, but it was her job. A job she had not because she'd inherited it, but because she owed everything she'd achieved, everything she'd acquired, to her don. And no matter how trepidatious she might be about facing Mikhail Petrov when she was convinced he was using her as a pawn in his feud with the family, she had never backed down from a fight and she wasn't about to start. "I'm not kidding. Nothing has changed. This is happening. Go and tell Michael. He'll want to beef up security for the family before the meeting—the house, the offices, Valentino's—assume no place is safe from attack. He'll know what to do. And let Don Carlo know I'm okay and I'll be over later."

Neal stood, understanding she was being dismissed. Siobhan sensed her reluctance to leave, but she needed a little alone time to get her emotions in check before she reviewed strategy with Carlo.

"I'll be with you at the meeting with Petrov," Neal said. "You shouldn't go in there alone."

She was right. She shouldn't meet Petrov alone, but she was resistant to the idea of bringing Neal with her. No matter that Petrov would likely be surrounded by his own security. He never went anywhere without his overly muscled bodyguards, but while his team was a show of force, for her, as a woman, having a bodyguard at her side signaled she was weak and needed protection. She needed to put Petrov on his heels if she was going to get any useful intel out of their meeting.

An idea flashed and her first instinct was to push it away, but as it rocked around inside her head, it became more and more intriguing. *Royal.* If she showed up to the meeting with Royal, Petrov would be distracted by the unfamiliar face—wondering who she was, what her presence meant. Whether she showed up with Neal or Royal, Petrov would scoff at the idea another woman could serve as protection, and Siobhan suspected he'd do so at his peril. Royal was strong and steady, and she'd pit her wits against Petrov and his men any day of the week. Bringing Royal along would be the perfect excuse to see her again and she realized that was a large part of her motivation. If she could accomplish two goals at once, why wouldn't she? Her skin tingled as she remembered Royal's hands on her naked body, focused on giving her pleasure and gently drawing out emotions she couldn't remember ever experiencing. Since the moment Royal had left, she'd wanted her back in her bed, but she'd settle for spending time with her, even if it was work. She should feel guilty about the possibility she was putting Royal in danger, but her instincts told her Royal didn't shy away from a challenge—a quality she found irresistible.

❖

Royal pushed through the door of the diner and walked directly to the counter, pleased to find several open spots on a busy Saturday morning. She placed the newspaper she'd brought on the counter to her left and looked at the waitress who'd appeared out of nowhere.

"Coffee?" she asked, slinging a cup and saucer in front of her as if an affirmative answer was a foregone conclusion.

Royal set her thumb on the saucer to keep it from rattling and checked the woman's name tag. Marge. Not because she intended to use it—she didn't want to draw attention—but gathering details was a habit. "Yes, black."

Marge nodded approvingly, took two steps, grabbed a steaming pot off of a burner, and filled her cup in one fluid motion. "You want a menu?"

"No need. I'll have eggs over easy, toast, bacon crisp."

Again with the nod and Marge was gone in a flash, the model of efficiency. She should take a page from Marge's book, but instead she'd completely mucked things up over the past twenty-four hours.

On any other job she'd be telling herself that sleeping with a potential target was a means to an end, and intimacy was one of the easiest ways to gather information. But she'd been trying to convince herself last night meant nothing since she'd left Siobhan's penthouse apartment, without success. She was distracted by Siobhan, intrigued by her role in the family, but more than that she was intrigued by the mystery of an accomplished woman who had an incredible amount going for her, but had chosen to dedicate her life to an organized crime family.

When she'd gotten back to her house last night, she'd scoured Siobhan's FBI file again. And again, but the facts hadn't changed. Raised by a single mother who worked at the Mancusos' mansion. She'd lived in the servants' quarters until her mother died suddenly when she was ten years old. Carlo Mancuso had literally taken her in. She'd moved into the big house, went to private school with his daughters, and to all appearances, she'd been a third daughter to him. She'd gone to college and law school at his behest and on his dime, dutifully come back to serve as his counselor, and armed with her knowledge of the law, she advised him on how to break it. To the FBI, she was as guilty as Carlo for all the crimes committed in the family name.

But as often happened in her line of work, when she met the players in person, Royal inevitably uncovered layers to all of the "bad" guys that showed they couldn't simply be reduced to their illegal activity. They had wives and families and other people who loved them. They were Little League coaches, food bank volunteers, and philanthropists. She replayed the image of Siobhan at the museum, discussing art and standing in front of the Dallas elite to deliver a message about charitable giving, looking nothing like a powerful counselor to Don Carlo Mancuso, one of the most notorious godfathers in Texas. Anyone would be a fool to underestimate her, but Royal had picked up on her tender side, first in the hesitation she'd shown about speaking to the crowd and then in bed where she'd been an incredibly receptive lover.

"May I borrow the sports section?"

She glanced to her left, surprised to see Wharton again. She'd expected him to send a low-level agent for a simple handoff. That he'd take the risk of appearing near her again meant he was unable to contain his excitement at what she'd managed to procure. "Sure," she said. She picked up the paper and swiped through the pages until she located a story about the Dallas Cowboys. She shook the section free and handed it to Wharton, slipping the flash drive into his hand with the transfer.

"I don't know what you're going to find in there. I wasn't able to read it." She'd tried to access the drive, but it was encrypted, and she'd eventually given up for fear she'd lock herself and worse yet, Siobhan, out of the data. She'd called Wharton and arranged this meet under the condition she would get the drive back by the end of the day, at which point she'd have to figure out a way to get it back into Siobhan's briefcase. She was torn between hoping there was something important on the drive and hoping it was nothing more than a backup of Siobhan's camera roll. While it would be great to have concrete evidence of Mancuso crimes, if the drive contained sensitive information about the family business, it was likely Siobhan was already looking for it. Royal had no idea how she was going to get it back to her, but she was anxious to do so as soon as possible.

"If it's okay with you, I'm going to take this back to my table," Wharton said, making a show of holding up the sports section. "I'll bring it back to you when I'm done."

She waved him off. "Keep it. I'm not big on sports."

He touched the brim of his hat, walked to a nearby table, and sat down in front of a huge stack of pancakes, which made Royal think of Ryan. Wharton had told her on the phone that all he'd been able to learn about Ryan was that his discharge was honorable—to Royal's relief—but he hadn't been able to find out what motivated it. Ryan had served four years of his five-year Ranger commitment. He may not have been the rule follower she'd always been, but she had a hard time coming up with a reason he'd break his promise to the Army when joining the service had been the sole source of solace for them both after the childhood they'd endured at the hands of a drunk man who couldn't keep his wife and didn't want to keep the kids she'd left behind.

The abuse they'd suffered, mostly verbal, but sometimes physical, had always affected Ryan worse. She'd shielded him the best she could, but keeping him fed, clothed, and housed was all she could manage when she had demons of her own to combat after raising them alone. But things were different now. She'd overcome her abandonment issues, and Ryan didn't need someone to provide creature comforts, but he did need emotional support and it was up to her to give it to him because he was never going to ask. If she were in the same circumstance, she probably wouldn't reach out for help either, so she could hardly blame him for trying to go it alone.

The waitress set her food down and the order was perfect. She hadn't realized she was hungry, and the bacon called out to her. She had a crispy piece halfway to her mouth when someone sat down in the chair next to her and leaned into her space. She broadened her shoulders to reassert her dominion, but the customer wasn't backing off. She dropped the bacon back down to her plate and prepared to do battle over the few inches between them, starting by "accidentally" slipping off her chair. When the stranger reached to break her fall, she took advantage of the diversion and shoved her setup down a space, but when she turned back to her, Royal realized it was Neal. "You're Siobhan's driver," she said, surprised and slightly alarmed to see her here with Wharton only a few feet away.

Neal's face twisted into a frown. "I'm more than her driver."

"You were there the day she almost got run down in the street." She left hanging the implication that she, not Neal was the one to lunge into action when Siobhan's life had been threatened, unsure whether needling her would work to her advantage.

"Yes, but you were closer. The entire family is grateful to you for your action."

She read the regret in Neal's creased brow, which confirmed she truly was dedicated to ensuring Siobhan's safety. It gave her a sense of peace to know Siobhan had someone close looking out for her, a realization that left her conflicted. Her concern for the target of her investigation was real, which on one hand was a good thing because it meant she was probably coming across as genuine to the Mancuso family. But it also meant she would have to contend with taking down the object of her affection, and for the first time in her career, the prospect was sour. What was it about Siobhan that made her stand out from other criminals she'd investigated?

Royal reflected on all of their interaction so far. Siobhan certainly conveyed a hard-edged exterior, but she'd seen enough glimpses of the tenderness beneath to know what she projected to the world wasn't the full picture. She'd been genuinely frightened after the near miss from the SUV and the bomb scare. And the day of the wedding, when Dominique had come on to her, she'd displayed a hint of jealousy, not the kind exhibited by someone who thought they had a right to the thing being fought over, but the kind expressed by someone who isn't sure they deserve the thing they want. Carlo's approval was obviously important to her, but not because she craved the power he conveyed to her, but because she didn't have a father of her own. There was a deep well there, and Royal knew she'd only begun to plumb its depths. She needed to know more about Siobhan's past to figure out her motivations for her current actions. She told herself it was for the job, but the truth was she simply wanted to know in order to be closer to Siobhan. If it helped her crack this case, then bonus.

"How else can I serve the family?" Royal asked, mostly motivated by the job she'd signed on to do.

"Come to the house tomorrow." Neal handed her a card. "You carry?"

She nodded.

"Leave it at home."

She read the information on the card and recognized the address for the Mancuso mansion. Two p.m. She wanted to ask if Siobhan would be there but knew this was a test to see if she would accept an assignment without question. "I'll be there."

"Good."

Neal lifted her coffee cup and drained it. She stood, towering over her, and tossed a five on the counter. Royal thought she was going to leave but she hesitated a moment.

"Is there something else?" she asked.

"She's important."

"I know."

"She has it in her head you're more suited to things than someone who's been with the family longer might be. You have any idea why that is?"

Royal studied her for a moment. Neal's conversational tone was likely deceptive and there was the possibility she was jealous of Royal's elevation in the ranks. She didn't want to rub it in, but she needed to establish her position without Neal feeling threatened because she sensed she might be useful to her later. "I pushed her out of the path of a moving car and I helped her escape the site of a potential bombing. It's possible she thinks I might be as qualified as the rest of her security team."

She clenched and unclenched her jaw, and then nodded slowly. "It's possible."

Royal raised her hands in surrender. "I'm not trying to get in your way here."

"See that you don't. If anything happens to her, it will affect many people. There could be war."

Royal was full of questions but tempered her curiosity for now. "I understand."

"Understand this. If anything happens to her, I will hold you personally responsible." She held her gaze for a moment, then abruptly turned and left without another word, leaving her with lots of questions. Had Neal seen Wharton with her, and if she had, did she detect the handoff of the flash drive? She resisted looking in Wharton's direction, but she was acutely conscious he was seated mere yards away, likely watching her entire exchange with Neal. She'd write a 302 detailing the encounter later, but right now all she could think about were Neal's words about Siobhan. *She's important.* To her? To the family? She sensed she meant more than her role as the Mancuso consigliere. Did the bodyguard have feelings for her charge? Did Siobhan return the affection?

She shook her head. She was acting like a jealous girlfriend. She could sleep with whoever she wanted while on the job, but feelings would only get in the way. She needed to get a handle on her distraction. When this job was over, she was going to take the vacation she'd dreamed about to a remote beach, and when she was good and rested, she might try to date for real. With secrets behind her, surely she'd be able to have some semblance of a normal life with a woman she wasn't trying to put in jail or hide her own secrets from.

She ate her meal slowly, watching for Wharton to leave and taking time to read the paper after he did. The words blurred on the page as curiosity ate at her with every passing moment. What did the Mancusos have in store for her tomorrow? But more importantly, would Siobhan be present for whatever was going down?

Chapter Fourteen

I don't like the idea of you going in there alone," Carlo said, patting Siobhan's arm.

It was Sunday afternoon, and they were both seated on the couch in his office, waiting for the others to arrive. Dominique had been scarce this morning, and Siobhan enjoyed the opportunity to spend some time with Carlo without D's caustic commentary in the background. Carlo had come out from behind his desk to sit beside her and, sitting so close, she noticed how much his illness had aged him. He hunched when he walked, like it was painful to stand fully upright, and his steps were slow and shuffled. She was meeting with Petrov in his place as a way of letting Petrov know he wasn't as important as he thought he was, but Carlo's weakened appearance was another reason to keep him out of the presence of their enemies who might be inclined to take advantage.

She gently squeezed his hand. "I appreciate your concern. I really do, but I won't be alone. Royal will be with me." Siobhan considered the matter a closed subject. She'd spent the last twenty-four hours thinking about the scheduled meeting with Petrov, and she wasn't afraid of whatever might go down. If Mikhail planned to kill her, he wasn't the type to have her walk into an ambush. That would be too messy for his taste. Either he showed up and listened to what she had to say, or this entire meeting would be a ruse of some kind and he would kill her later. Her money was on the former. He would be curious about why they'd scheduled the meeting and why she was there instead of Carlo, and she believed he'd listen long enough to satisfy his curiosity. As for her safety after the meet? That would be up to Neal and Michael and the rest of the Mancuso team to handle. She'd never dwelled on her safety in the past, and she wasn't going to start now. She was already older than her mother was when she'd died—every year from here on out was a bonus.

Besides, Royal would be with her. She couldn't quite explain what had motivated her to ask for Royal as her escort other than she thought it would be disconcerting to Petrov, but she felt confident and safe on her arm and perhaps that was enough. But tagging Royal for this mission would put her in harm's way too. Was it fair to take her along?

"You like this woman," Carlo said.

It was disturbing—his ability to see her thoughts, cut to the heart of what was bothering her. She supposed it was one of the traits that made him a good don, but to her it was more than that. He was the closest thing to a father she'd ever had, and although she'd always known Celia and Dominique would be the ones who inherited the Mancuso empire, she knew she held a special place in Carlo's heart, and he would make sure she was cared for even after he was gone. She suspected him asking about Royal was part of that.

"She is very capable. I think she will make a good addition to your organization."

Carlo frowned. "It is always business with you, but life is about more than how you earn your money. Money is a means to an end. It's how we afford safety and security and power, but it is not a substitute for love and family. Money gives you the freedom to have these things, but if you don't take the time to enjoy the fruits of your labor, you will die, old and alone, with strangers squabbling over your estate."

"You think I should get married like Celia?"

He waved his hand. "Celia is my daughter and I love her, but she married a man who will be a foot soldier, never a leader. You would never be satisfied with someone who doesn't rise to your level. Whoever you choose must be smart and fearless and passionate about you, but you must let them be close to you in both heart and mind or it will never work. I had a great love, but I lost it because I put power before passion. It was necessary, or I thought it was at the time, but I believe now I made poor choices. An old man looks back on his past through the lens of experience and sees much that was clouded from his view before. You do not have to marry, but you should choose a partner who is your soul mate who loves you fiercely and wants to build a life with you."

Siobhan had never heard him speak this way before. Celia and Dominique's mother had died when they were all teenagers and she had very few memories of her other than she and Carlo never displayed affection in public, but she'd always figured that was Carlo's way of maintaining a semblance of power even in his role as husband. Now she wondered if there had been a rift between them brought about by his split loyalty between his insular family and the larger family that made up the Mancuso empire. Whatever it was, he was acting like someone whose days were numbered, reflecting on his past, and she wanted to divert this conversation before she started to tear up.

"Thank you for the advice, but my first allegiance will always be to you. This is not the time to be distracted by emotions."

He studied her for an uncomfortable moment. "You may be right. We will speak of your future another time. But today, you must be careful because if Petrov sees what I do, your new friend may be a vulnerability you cannot afford. You should not lose her before you have explored your options."

Her stomach turned at his echo of her thoughts from earlier. Was it fair to put Royal in danger in order to assuage her own desire to have her by her side?

A knock on the door interrupted her thoughts. "Come in," Carlo called out.

Michael cracked the door. "She's here."

This was it. If she was going to change her mind, this was the moment to do it. She met Carlo's eyes. What would he do?

"Bring her in," he said, answering her silent question. He waited until Michael left to say more. "Let her make the choice. Her response will tell you everything you need to know."

A moment later, Royal walked into the room, her eyes searching until they landed on Siobhan. Siobhan met her steady gaze, startled once again by the intensity of their connection, but she kept quiet and let Carlo take the lead.

"Have a seat," he said, pointing to the chair across from them, as if they had all the time in the world for a friendly chat.

Royal complied, and in the intervening silence, Siobhan took a moment to assess this woman who'd completely captivated her from the moment of their first meeting. Royal was dashing as usual in charcoal gray slacks and a black shirt and stylish black sports coat. Her shirt was open at the collar, and Siobhan's mind flashed to the memory of kissing her way up the side of Royal's taut neck while she moaned against her touch.

What was wrong with her? She'd never let another woman occupy her thoughts to this degree, and right now it was imperative that she be free from distractions. She'd been planning to let Carlo take the lead, but instead she did what she always did when she needed to be free of emotions that threatened to overwhelm her—she plunged right into the work. "We have a job for you if you are interested."

Royal nodded slowly. "I wouldn't be here if I wasn't interested. I may have chosen to work in a field that doesn't use all of my capabilities, but that doesn't mean I have lost my skills."

Had she heard extra emphasis on the word "skills," or was she imagining things? Siobhan had carefully cultivated her intuition, but Royal had shattered it into pieces the moment she'd broken through her bricked up outer wall.

"Tell me about these skills," Carlo asked.

Royal settled back against the chair, signaling she was confident in what she was about to say. "Once upon a time, I was an Army Ranger. My expertise was munitions, but I am equally skilled at hand-to-hand combat."

Siobhan knew she was telling the truth. After she'd told Carlo every detail of how Royal had hustled her out of the museum and had experience with explosives, Carlo had arranged to obtain Royal's military record from one of his contacts. Siobhan suspected part of why he'd done so was to determine if she might've had anything to do with the bomb threat, but Royal's file revealed she was everything she said and more. She'd earned several honors, including a commendation medal.

"It seems then you'd have no trouble protecting yourself," Carlo said, "but my immediate concern is your willingness to protect someone precious to me."

Royal looked directly at Siobhan as she answered him. "I can see why you'd want to make sure she remains safe. She is indeed of great value and I do not take her trust in me for granted."

Siobhan stared back at Royal. No one had ever spoken to her like this and she wasn't sure how to react. Royal said all the right things, treated her tenderly like a lover, yet she couldn't quite accept she was for real. She suspected her reticence was because she didn't think she deserved it, but even if she didn't deserve it, she loved the way Royal's loyalty and affection made her feel. Was that enough to let her get close?

❖

Royal centered her concentration on Siobhan while simultaneously trying to read the room. When Neal had approached her yesterday, she'd wondered if she'd been sent to find out if she had the flash drive, but it was pretty clear the Mancuso family's focus was trained on her for some other reason. Still, she'd brought the drive with her today, hoping she'd find an opportunity to put it back where she'd found it. Michael had given her a thorough pat down when she'd arrived, but the drive was fastened deep into the inner lining of her jacket, near her chest, and she found men generally were pussies when it came to patting down a woman's chest, thank God. When she'd entered the room, she'd spotted Siobhan's bag sitting next to her, and she'd been plotting how she could return the drive without being noticed, but since she'd been under the laser focus of Carlo's attention upon entering the room, that mission would have to wait.

Everyone she'd come into contact with at the mansion today had been circumspect about the reason for her visit, and her only clue about what they had planned for her was Neal's implication that Siobhan might be in danger and she would be tasked with keeping her safe. While she appreciated the confidence and had no doubt she was up to the task, she couldn't help but wonder why Neal or that beefy moose

Michael weren't able to guard her on their own. "What is this new job?"

Siobhan glanced at Carlo who motioned for her to answer. "Mikhail Petrov is the head of a powerful family here in Dallas. There was a time, not that long ago, when our business interests aligned, but he took advantage of our hospitality and we no longer have mutual interests."

Royal nodded, careful to keep her expression neutral, although hearing Petrov's name put all of her senses on high alert. She, like any law enforcement officer based in Dallas, had heard of Petrov and his organization. His primary enterprise was prostitution, but unlike some of the other prostitution rings in the area, his relied on unwilling participants who'd been trafficked for the sole purpose of building his empire. He was a scourge, and federal agents had tried without success to penetrate his organization and bring him down. The idea that whatever the Mancusos had planned for today might have something to do with Petrov had her ramped up, but she hid her excitement because Royal Flynn, bar services manager from Houston, wouldn't have any reason to either know who Petrov was or understand the significance. Instead, she ventured a question. "Are you at war with this Petrov character?"

"Yes." Siobhan cleared her throat. "The day we met, when that SUV tried to run me down? We have reason to believe he gave the order. We also have reason to believe he was responsible for several hits on our business interests since, and the bomb at the museum."

Royal shook her head in disbelief. "And you think he's going to try again? Are you going after him?"

"We are," Siobhan said, "But not in the way you think. I'm meeting with him today to deliver a warning. We do not start war lightly, and it's in everyone's best interest if he chooses to back off on his own."

Royal wanted to reach over and take Siobhan's hand in hers. Her life had been threatened twice yet no one in the Mancuso family was willing to deliver immediate retribution. Instead, they were going to send his potential victim in to visit with him, like injecting blood in shark-infested waters and lowering a cage with his favorite meal. What would happen after Petrov tore Siobhan into pieces? Would that be enough to justify real action? If Dominique or Celia had been threatened, she suspected hellfire would rein down on Petrov—no questions asked.

"You have a problem with this plan?" Carlo asked.

Damn, she'd let her feelings show. She needed to be more careful. She took a deep breath and asked for permission to speak freely.

"Of course, I expect the people who work for me to speak their mind," Carlo said.

Royal wondered if that was entirely true and if there would be some punishment for pushing back, but sharp concern for Siobhan's well-being meant she had to take him at his word. "I would expect a direct threat to be met by a direct action. If this Petrov is a threat, it seems the best course of action would be to take him out before he can do further harm."

Carlo and Siobhan exchanged looks, but Royal couldn't get a read on what they were thinking. "Please forgive me," she said. "I have overstepped. Of course, you have your reasons, and I'm happy to serve you in whatever capacity you request."

"We do have our reasons," Carlo said. "Siobhan will tell you what you need to know. Are you willing to accompany her to this meeting? She will not have anyone else with her there and I will be relying on you to keep her safe."

It was an odd ask, but there was no way Royal was going to say no to the opportunity to be the first federal agent to get close to Petrov, ever. "Of course. I will do whatever you want, not just because you've asked, but because I don't want any harm to come to Siobhan."

"Legend has it once you save someone's life, they are your charge for life," Carlo said with the hint of a smile. "Are you willing to accept this burden?"

"It is no burden to me." Royal turned to Siobhan and injected as much sincerity as she could into her next words. "It would be my honor to accompany you."

Siobhan's expression remained impassive, but Royal spotted a hint of emotion in her eyes. Did she really want to meet Petrov with Royal as her only protection or was she doing it to please the old man? The real question was why did she care so much about the safety of a woman she was charged with bringing down?

"Excellent," Siobhan said. "We should get going. Neal will drive us, but only you and I will enter Petrov's compound." She stood and assisted Carlo to his feet, a tender moment that illustrated his vulnerability and age in a way Royal doubted many people ever witnessed, and she was tempted to look away to allow them to share this tender father-daughter-like moment.

She rode in the back of the Suburban with Siobhan, conscious of the fact the partition between the front and back seat was open. "What's the plan when we get there?"

"I don't have one," Siobhan said. "Not a single one, anyway. My plan is to get a message across to Petrov that his threats and continued assaults on our business will not be tolerated."

"And you think he'll be receptive?"

"I think he'll be an ass. My research says he's mystified by powerful women. Most of the women he comes into contact with are the prostitutes he farms out to the rich and powerful. Kneeling, on their backs—those are the positions he's used to women occupying. He doesn't understand someone like Carlo, who relies on the advice of his daughter and has a female consigliere."

"So, your strategy is to knock him off his game," Royal said. "And you figured adding another woman to the mix would add to the effect."

"Something like that. I also want him to know I'm not afraid of him. Sending someone to tell him to stop threatening me would convey the exact opposite message."

Royal glanced at Neal, who was consulting directions on her phone, and said in a low voice, "And here I hoped you invited me along because you wanted to see me again." She traced a finger lightly along Siobhan's thigh.

Siobhan batted her hand away. "You shouldn't thank me until we're on the way home. This visit could be dangerous."

"I don't scare easily."

"Fear is healthy. It means you value life."

Royal rolled the thought over in her head. Siobhan had a point. She'd experienced fright many times in her career, but it was the will to live that got her past her fears and safely out the other side. She'd been certain she was going to die at Danny's hand just a few weeks ago, but the fear had motivated her to do whatever it took to get out of the van and away from danger. Lucky for her, fate had intervened in the form of an oncoming bus. Every time she'd been afraid of dying, she'd come out the other side, alive and well. Most people emerged from circumstances like hers with a new lease on life, but she'd merely escaped ready to face death again. What did that say about her?

A few minutes later, Neal turned the Suburban off the road and onto a gravel road that appeared to lead into the woods. "Where are we?" Royal asked, a little embarrassed she hadn't paid closer attention to the route.

"Rockwall. His place is on the lake. About a quarter mile up ahead."

Royal kept her eyes trained on the path, determined to pay close and careful attention to every detail from here on out. She might have nine lives, but Siobhan might not be so lucky, and she took the oath she'd made to Carlo seriously. She told herself making promises to mob bosses was part of the role, but the truth was she really did care about Siobhan. She was more vulnerable than she let on, and Royal wanted to protect that part of her and keep her safe from harm. If that meant she was more risk-averse than normal, so be it, but at the end of the meeting with Petrov, Siobhan was going to walk out of there unharmed. No matter what.

CHAPTER FIFTEEN

Siobhan listened as Neal negotiated with the guard at the gate who wanted her to drop them off and come back later.

"That wasn't the deal," Neal said. "I'll wait in the car, but I'm not leaving Ms. Collins here without a ride home."

The guard leaned in and looked in the back seat. He pointed at Royal. "Who is this?"

Siobhan saw Royal start to answer, but she beat her to it. "She's with me. I told your boss that I wouldn't be alone. Surely he has people of his own he will want to have in the room when we speak. He can't possibly think I wouldn't want the same."

"Hold on." He ducked back out the window, and she watched him make a call. Although he spoke in Russian, she was sure she could surmise the content of the conversation. A moment later, he stuck his head back in the window.

"Okay, you," he pointed at Neal, "stay in the car. Park to the right of the main building." He didn't mention Royal, and Siobhan assumed it was because whoever he'd spoken to had confirmed what she said. She breathed a sigh of relief, glad she wouldn't have to enter Petrov's complex alone.

The ride to the house was bumpy but quick, considering it felt like they were miles from the road in this remote location. Truthfully, they were fairly close to roads and other civilization. Unlike many of his lakefront neighbors, Petrov had left much of the greenbelt intact, giving the illusion of seclusion.

Royal stepped out of the SUV first and helped her down. Neal rolled down the driver's side window.

"I'll be close by if you need me," she said. She pointed at Siobhan's bag in the back seat. "Do you want to take that?"

Siobhan shook her head. "No. I don't want Petrov's men searching my things. And don't worry. I'm glad you're here, but we'll be fine," she said, tossing her a bone. She knew it had to grate on her that she'd chosen Royal to accompany her, but she couldn't let feelings factor into her strategy. She glanced back at Royal and amended the thought, acknowledging feelings might have already wound their way in.

She watched Neal drive off and park in a spot about fifty feet from the front door of the large, plain concrete building. She knew from Google Earth there were several more buildings behind this one. So far, she wasn't impressed—the complex was ugly compared to the Mancuso mansion, but she would reserve judgment until they were inside.

A butler met them at the door. Well, that was one thing Petrov and Carlo had in common. He told them to wait in the foyer and marched out of the room to report their arrival.

The cavernous foyer looked like a small ballroom, and it was almost as big as her apartment. The edges of the room were decorated with ornate statues and gaudy paintings, including an enormous portrait of Mikhail Petrov seated on a horse with a pack of dogs along beside. The whole room was a museum curated by a drunk hero worshipper, and it told her Petrov surrounded himself with people who told him what he wanted to hear—a fact that didn't bode well for their meeting.

But in the meantime, she could appreciate the grandeur of

the place. Any moment she expected to see a couple glide by, dancing to a classic waltz. She remembered how, when she was a small child, her mother had danced with her in the kitchen, replicating the dances from the fancy parties Mrs. Mancuso had thrown when she'd been alive. Mrs. Mancuso hadn't been very friendly to her, but she did let her join Dominique and Celia when they got to stay up late and watch portions of their parents' extravagant parties. Dominique made fun of the guests, but Siobhan was riveted by the spectacle of their finery and festive dances.

"Are you okay?"

She looked up into Royal's eyes to see them full of concern. "Of course. Why do you ask?"

"You looked like you were very far away just now," Royal whispered. "If you don't want to do this, we can leave."

Siobhan took a moment to consider her answer. What she wanted to say was that no sane person would be "up for this," but the admission was too telling to make while they were here in Petrov's home where anyone could be listening in. "No," she replied, purposefully making her tone brisk. "I do want to be here, and I hope you do too."

Royal didn't have time to answer before the butler reappeared and ushered them farther into the house. The hallways were filled with more tributes to Petrov and Russian culture, and by the time the butler stopped in front of the door where presumably Petrov was waiting, she'd had her fill.

"Mr. Petrov is waiting for you," the butler said and opened the door with a flourish.

The room was as gaudy as the rest of the house. A large white bearskin rug was in the center of the room and Petrov, wearing a sharply tailored forest green suit, was seated on a gold chair that looked suspiciously like a throne. He rose as they entered. "Come in, come in. It is my honor to be your host."

Whatever she'd been expecting, Siobhan had not anticipated the friendly greeting, and it almost caught her off guard. Almost. She took his hand and stared him directly in the eyes. "Hello, Mikhail. It's been a long time."

"It has, and much has changed since our last meeting." He jerked his chin in Royal's direction. "Who is this? Another family member who is not actually part of the family?"

She bit back a smart retort, instead motioning for Royal to step forward. "This is Royal Flynn. She is my protege. I brought her with me today to learn how one handles a difficult situation. I knew you wouldn't mind."

"Of course not. I too brought friends to our meeting." He gestured to the back of the room where two large men stood guard. "I knew *you* wouldn't mind."

She smiled and dipped her head to acknowledge the touché.

He raised a tall, thin glass filled with a clear liquid that she suspected was vodka. How cliché. "Would you like a drink?"

She would. She'd like an entire bottle, but she wasn't about to take a drink from someone known to use poison to kill his enemies, plus she wanted to remain sharp. "Another time, perhaps. I have a lot of work to do today."

"What a shame to spend a Sunday working." He motioned to two chairs arranged in front of his. "Have a seat. Let us discuss the reason for your visit. Have the Mancusos finally changed their mind about our business arrangement?"

She sat in one of the chairs and watched Royal cautiously settle into her seat. She could feel Royal's tense, raw energy from several feet away, and she wanted to reach out to her, reassure her she was used to dealing with bullies like Petrov.

They weren't much different from the federal prosecutors who often wielded their power like blunt instruments in their attempt to beat defendants into submission. She'd learned to combat these practices by being smarter and better prepared since the law was often not on her side. "I'm not here to discuss business arrangements. Did your people not inform you of the reason for this visit?" She added extra inflection at the end of her question to signal she considered his people to have failed him by not preparing him for this meeting.

He laughed. "They did, but I did not believe them because what they told me was so incredulous. You have started a rumor that I tried to run you down in the street, raided several of your businesses, and then placed a bomb at a social event. You must think I have nothing else to do but pursue you. Are you that important to the Mancuso family?"

That was a good question, and she wasn't sure she knew the answer. Carlo relied on her counsel more so now than before he'd become ill. If she wasn't there to take charge, would Dominique step up or would she stay in her role as the petulant child? D was certainly capable. She knew everything Siobhan knew, and being in charge of the books meant she had an added in with the organization, as if she needed one since she carried the Mancuso name.

She decided to ignore Petrov's question. "If it's not you, then who is it?"

He raised his shoulders in an exaggerated motion. "I have no idea, but perhaps if I were to find out for you, you might be more amenable to reopening a discussion about how we may work together. I have many contacts I can put to use if I believe doing so would reward us both."

She studied him carefully. He had as many reasons to lie to her as he did to make this outlandish offer. The purpose of her visit today wasn't to get him to tell her the truth, but to issue a warning. But what if he wasn't the one responsible for the attacks? It would be foolish to pass on the opportunity to put his intel to use, and as much as she wanted to tell him to fuck off, she wanted his information more. Stringing him along would be dangerous business, but no more dangerous than not pursuing every lead. "If you are lying, we will crush you."

He raised his almost empty glass and laughed again, but this time his laughter fell flat in the face of her threat. "You had better hope you never have to make good on that promise." He set the glass down and leaned forward. "I'm feeling generous today, so I will assume you didn't mean any harm to me but were merely speaking out of frustration. I will provide you with answers and you will reconsider our arrangement. If not, perhaps I will have to go into business with whoever it is that is set on bringing your little empire down."

She stood and tossed her card on the coffee table in front of his faux throne. "You have forty-eight hours to contact me with verifiable information." She snapped her fingers at Royal, who hopped to her feet, and then she said her good-bye to Petrov accentuated by a sharp jab of her index finger. "We're done. For now."

❖

Royal followed Siobhan to the Suburban, resisting the urge to check her six on the way out of Petrov's concrete palace. She knew Siobhan's finger snapping was all part of the show she was putting on for Petrov, but damn if her show of power wasn't sexy.

Neal started the car as they approached, and within moments, they were out of the compound and on the highway back to Dallas.

"Thoughts?" Siobhan asked.

Royal had been examining the content of Siobhan's conversation with Petrov since they'd walked out of his fur-lined drawing room, and she couldn't deny he'd seemed sincere. Her instincts told her Petrov knew more than he was letting on, but if he did already know the identity of who had it in for the Mancusos, why wouldn't he go ahead and share that information as a kind of olive branch to get them to agree to revisit their business arrangement? She could think of two reasons: he really was the culprit, or he didn't think Siobhan had the power to close the deal on the spot. If it was the latter, then he'd want her to go back and get Carlo's buy-in before handing over valuable intel. And if he thought that, then why would he also think that taking Siobhan out would be a huge blow to the family? "He doesn't think you have the power that you do. Or that you speak for the family."

"What is that supposed to mean?"

Royal led her through her logic. "I believe that he didn't target the family, at least not on his own. But I think he's testing the waters to find out who's really in charge. Does he know that Carlo is ill?"

Siobhan shot a look at the front of the Suburban, but the partition was up and Neal appeared to be fully focused on the road. "How do you know Carlo is ill?"

Royal scrunched her face. "Because I have eyes. Besides the wedding, when was the last time he appeared in public?"

Siobhan looked distressed. "He doesn't leave the mansion much anymore. He can still get around, but his body pays the price for several days after a lot of exertion. The wedding took a lot out of him."

Royal reached for Siobhan's hand and intertwined their fingers, wanting to comfort her, tell her everything would be all right, but that would be a lie, so instead she merely said, "I doubt anyone at the wedding noticed. He looked like he was having a great time. What does he have?"

"Liver cancer. It was slow at first, but it has progressed in the past few months."

"Who else knows?"

"You mean besides you?" Siobhan offered a rueful smile. "Dominique. Michael. Salvadore. I expect some other members of the house staff have figured out he hasn't been feeling well, but I doubt they know exactly what's going on." She pointed at the partition. "Neal probably knows, but I haven't told her. She's observant."

Royal filed that fact away. "Celia doesn't know?"

"No. He wanted us to keep it from her. With the wedding and all…"

Siobhan's voice trailed off, and Royal wanted to scoop her in her arms, kiss her head, and tell her everything would be okay. But Siobhan wasn't a small child in need of comfort. She was a grown woman who had to make peace with this in her own way, but at the first sign she wanted comforting, Royal was determined to be there.

"I think Petrov knows. He may not have the specifics, but someone has told him enough for him to believe there is a shift in power or there's going to be. It may be in your best interest to align with him now before someone else does."

"Who would that someone be?"

"I don't know. Some other family who wants to edge in on your businesses?"

"Maybe." Siobhan shook her head. "I have to think this through."

"We're almost back at the mansion. Carlo may have some ideas."

"No."

"No?"

"I don't want to bother him with this until I'm sure I've explored every angle." Siobhan tapped her fingers on the armrest.

"I'm a decent sounding board if you're interested." Royal reached for her hand. "Have Neal take us to your place," she said, thinking she would have the best chance of returning the flash drive if they were there, but also wanting to spend some time alone with her. "You can call Carlo from there and I can get my car later or we can get someone to bring it." She released Siobhan's hand, but didn't pull away. "Strictly business. If that's what you want."

"I'm not sure what I want."

"You don't need to decide right now, but it's your call. Whenever you make up your mind."

Siobhan stared down at their hands and laced her fingers through Royal's. "Okay." She rapped on the partition until Neal lowered it a few inches. "Change of plans. We're going to my place. Please get Pete to take Royal's car to her house, and I'll take her home later."

Neal nodded, but Royal could tell by the tight set of her jaw she had opinions about the change in plans, but thankfully, she didn't butt in with an opposing opinion.

Siobhan called Carlo from the car and gave him a curtailed version of their visit with Petrov, basically telling him it had been impossible to tell if Petrov was telling the truth about not being involved in the attacks on her or their business interests, but she'd delivered the threat either way. When they reached her apartment building, Neal turned into the parking garage instead of the valet stand.

"Don't even argue," she said. "I'll leave you alone, but I need to walk through the apartment and make sure it's safe before I do. Five, ten minutes tops."

Royal didn't want her there, but she appreciated the care

she took to protect Siobhan and wasn't about to argue the point. Neal entered the apartment first and was inside for a moment before reappearing at the door to let Siobhan know it was okay to enter.

"Your room's clear. I'll only be a few minutes with the rest of the place."

Siobhan turned to Royal. "I need to use the bathroom. I'll be right back."

Royal watched as she walked through the small foyer and set her bag on the same table where Royal had found it when she left the apartment the morning before. Now if she could distract Neal for a few minutes, she'd have her chance. When Siobhan disappeared into the master suite, she called out to Neal. "I'll check in here if you want to check the kitchen and study."

"Okay," she called out from the dining room.

Royal glanced around while she fished the drive out of her jacket. Satisfied this was the best opportunity she'd have, she reached into Siobhan's bag and felt around for the zippered pocket. Yesterday, the bag had been only partly full, but today it was stuffed, and she had to shove the contents aside before she could find the compartment she was looking for while keeping an eye out for Neal. She reached for the pull and started to ease it open when she heard footfalls getting closer. She pulled her hand out and left it hovering over the bag while she looked down the hall toward Siobhan's room, but the door was closed and there was no sign of Siobhan. She heard the footfalls again. Shit. She knew what was happening, but she resisted the urge to whirl around.

"Hey, what are you doing?"

In one fluid move, she opened her hand and dropped the flash drive into the bag, grabbed the handle and pushed it close to the wall. She turned to Neal, careful to keep her face and tone neutral. "Just checking back here." She pointed at the glowing lamp on the table. "Do you know if this was on when Siobhan left her place this morning?"

Neal stared at her for a moment and looked at the bag and back to her. She stayed still, hoping she looked natural, but fearing she'd raised her suspicion.

"It's on a timer," she said. "Smart plug."

She nodded slowly, thankful for the opening. "Are there more smart plugs in the house? Do you have them secured?"

"Do we have what secured?" Siobhan asked as she walked out of the master suite down the hall toward where they were standing.

Royal pointed at the outlet where the lamp was plugged in. "Neal and I were talking about how smart plugs are convenient, but they provide an entry point for hackers. They could potentially get access to your home network, install listening devices and other things." She looked back at Neal. "How often do you do a thorough sweep?"

"Daily. Unless she's been home all day," she said, looking unsettled. "We did one this morning."

"And she's been gone all afternoon," Royal pointed out. "I'll do another sweep now, but I think you should add another anytime she's out of the house for more than an hour."

"How about you two start talking *to* me rather than about me?" Siobhan said. "I'm hungry. How does Thai sound?"

Royal and Neal both stared at her as if she'd asked them to perform complex math. Neal was the first to respond. "I should go. Royal can check for bugs and I'll double-check in the morning." She edged toward the door. "Call me if you need me."

When the door shut behind her, Royal breathed a sigh of relief.

"Everything okay?" Siobhan asked.

"Releasing pent-up stress. I guess I didn't realize how worried I was about going to Petrov's."

"You didn't seem scared."

"I wasn't. Not for me anyway. You, on the other hand, I was definitely concerned for you."

Siobhan reached for her hand and pulled her close. "I'm fine."

Royal ran a hand down her side. Siobhan had changed from her suit into a pair of black silk lounge pants, and her loose-fitting top allowed ready access to her smooth skin. "Yes, yes, you are."

"Why don't you take me to bed and show me how fine you think I am."

Royal grinned. "I thought you were hungry What about my Thai food?"

Siobhan arched away from her. "If that's what you'd rather have..." She took two steps toward the bedroom and looked back over her shoulder. "But if you're really hungry, I'll be in here."

CHAPTER SIXTEEN

Royal was standing in the warehouse behind Valentino's when her phone buzzed with a text from Siobhan.

If you really really still want Thai food, come over tonight.

She smiled at the reference. They never had gotten around to ordering food last night.

"You get a match on Grindr or something?" Robert asked. He raised his hands in the air when she flipped him off. "Doesn't bother me that you're queer. Everybody has their thing, but we're never going to finish here if you keep checking your phone."

"What am I supposed to do? I can't help it if I'm popular." Royal typed a quick reply to Siobhan's text and shoved her phone in her pocket. It had been difficult to leave Siobhan's bed this morning, but having to show up to do inventory with Robert was added cruelty. The guy didn't believe in the pleasure of silence, preferring instead to fill every moment with stories about how he'd worked his way up the chain of command with the Mancusos.

"So, like I was saying," he said, continuing his tale as if there had been no interruption, "with there being no sons, I imagine old man Mancuso will be looking for someone to carry on the family business when he's gone."

Whoa. Royal kept her eyes trained on the clipboard she was using to record numbers to keep him from seeing her incredulous expression. She'd figured out Robert was full of himself within a few minutes of their first meeting, but this was next level. "And you think you're that guy?" she asked, careful to keep her voice casual.

"I'm as good as anyone. It's not like I think he's going to just hand it over to someone, but Dominique is single. Don't you know whoever she marries is going to be first in line."

He was either completely clueless or diabolical. "What about Tony, Celia's husband? He's first in. Don't you think he has a better shot at being in charge?"

Robert laughed. "Tony's a pussy. He wasn't 'allowed' to have a stripper at his bachelor party—that's how whipped he is. You think he's going to be in charge of anything?"

"Hey, I don't know all these people like you."

"You know some better than others."

Royal's senses went on alert. "What's that supposed to mean?"

"Word is you're getting some from that hot piece lawyer. What's she like? I hear those icy ones are real pillow princesses."

Royal barely heard his last few words and he was barely able to say them. She grabbed his shirt in both hands and slammed him up against one of the tall racks of booze. The bottles shook and teetered, but she didn't give a shit if they all fell down and crashed glass around them. He grabbed her hands, but she tightened her grip, cutting off his air supply until he started beating her arms with his fists.

"Let me go," he choked out.

She released her grip, and he sagged against the rack, knocking over a few bottles of Frangelico. The large broken pieces of glass rolled away, leaving only the cloying odor of the liqueur and the crunch of glass as he stepped through it trying to get away from her.

"What the hell was that about?" he yelled.

"Does Don Carlo know how you talk about his consigliere?"

He waved a hand dismissively. "What? You going to go rat me out?"

"I might."

"Why would you want to do that?"

"I have ambitions of my own. If Don Carlo finds out you're an overly ambitious piece of shit, he may decide I'm a better choice to move up the ranks."

"You'll never be made. You don't have what it takes."

"Because I'm not Italian? Because I'm not a man?" She smiled. "But see here—I have something you don't. Respect for the things and people that are important to Carlo Mancuso. All you have is naked ambition. We'll see which one of us he's more likely to favor."

"Right. The day I marry Dominique, you can forget about any ambition you have. You'll be out."

Her phone buzzed again, and she decided answering it right there in front of him was the perfect way to show her defiance. She checked the screen. It was another text, but this time it wasn't from Siobhan. She scanned it and shoved her phone back in her pocket. "I have to go."

"We're not done here."

She shrugged. "Can't be helped. I have other responsibilities."

He yelled at her, cursing, as she walked away. She'd probably overplayed her hand, leading him to believe Siobhan or Carlo had summoned her when it would be easy for him to find out that wasn't the case. The text had been code from Wharton, demanding immediate contact and complete discretion. She wouldn't call him from this phone, but she needed to find a place to make the call out of the earshot of anyone connected to the Mancusos because Wharton only ever used this code when something serious was up. Her mind went immediately to the contents of the flash drive. Had he found something important there?

She drove home and walked to a laundromat down the street. She'd scoped it out when she'd first moved in and learned it was one of only a handful of places in the city that still had a pay phone. Wharton answered on the fifth ring, right as she'd been about to hang up.

"What took you so long to answer?" she asked. "I'd expect you to be waiting by the phone after that text."

"We have a lot going on here."

His words were clipped, and she got the distinct impression he was annoyed. Well, fuck that. He'd been the one to contact her. "Tell me about it. What's up?"

"I'm pulling you in."

Royal heard him clearly, but his words didn't make sense. "Say again?"

"You're off the case. Come in today. We'll do a quick debrief and then you can take that vacation you're always threatening."

"Wait." She leaned her head against the phone as she tried to process what was going on. Was this because she'd slept with Siobhan? No, he'd practically asked her to do that when he begged her to take this case. Was her cover blown? No, if that were true, he'd tell her that so she'd know exactly how to extricate. Her stomach roiled. If it wasn't one of those things… "Tell me why."

"The flash drive gave us everything we need. The director

doesn't want to risk an agent when we don't need to and I've been ordered to bring you in. It's as simple as that."

"It's not that simple. I'm close to a break. I've developed trust with these people. I can't just leave now," she said, trying to keep the desperation out of her voice.

"Don't fight me on this. Hell, you didn't even want this case," he replied, his voice weary with frustration.

"It's not that simple. Give me a week." She waited for a response, but when a dial tone was the only reply, she realized he'd hung up the phone, and she slammed the handset against the base in frustration. What the hell had been on that drive and how could it be conclusive enough to justify yanking her out of an undercover assignment? *One you didn't want in the first place.*

It was true and she hadn't needed him to remind her. She had resisted taking this gig, but like every other one before it, she'd quickly settled into her new identity and become consumed with solving the puzzle, and this one was particularly intriguing because Siobhan played a part. That Wharton would yank her back to real life before she'd even had a chance to put together the full picture was unprecedented.

She walked the short distance back to her house—make that Royal Flynn's house—and sat down in the living room to consider her options, which were few. She could walk out of the house with nothing except the clothes on her back, find a ride back to her apartment across town, and resume her regularly scheduled life, or she could defy Wharton's orders and keep working undercover. What would the bureau do if she chose the latter? Would they burn her or leave her in place to bolster their investigation? She was a big fan of asking for forgiveness rather than permission, but she usually did so from a place of power. If she chose to stay in the role she'd assumed, she risked being left without a safety net, and if the FBI chose to burn her, she might be risking her life by continuing to pretend to be someone she wasn't.

She needed time to figure out what to do, and she needed to start by reviewing all of her notes. She walked into her bedroom closet and yanked the rope for the pull-down ladder to the attic. The metal box was exactly where she'd left it when she'd replaced it on Saturday, after stowing the burner phone she'd used to make a copy of the flash drive. She grabbed her notes, stared at the phone for a moment and then grabbed it too. She placed the notes and the phone into her pocket and climbed back down. Before she settled in to review her notes, she pulled her gun out of her nightstand drawer and checked the clip. Wharton hadn't said she was in direct danger, but foreboding stirred in her gut and she needed to plan for every contingency.

She'd no sooner sat down to read her notes than her phone rang. Half expecting it to be Wharton asking why she wasn't home yet, she checked the screen and saw Siobhan's number displayed. She was torn. If she didn't answer and Siobhan wanted her for a job, she'd wonder where she was. If Siobhan wanted her for something more intimate, she might be more forgiving about the lack of response. Either way, she wasn't sure what to say if she did answer. "Hey, can you hang on a few minutes while I try to figure out why I'm no longer supposed to be spying on you?"

Feeling like a coward, she let the call go to voice mail and returned her attention to the notes spread out in front of her, but as many times as she read them, she kept coming back to the flash drive. Finally, she scooped up the whole lot of info, her gun, her wallet. She put on a ball cap and sunglasses and took off on foot.

The nearest bus stop was a block away. She waited with a few other stragglers until the big yellow and white DART bus approached, and she let everyone else in front of her so she could be last to board. She asked the driver a few questions about the route and settled into a seat near the front, careful to keep her head tucked low and her face out of sight. A few miles later, she got off the bus at the train station and selected her route again, taking several lines around the city before abandoning the train for a short walk back to her apartment building.

She stared at the small complex from a distance, wondering if anyone was watching, and finally deciding if they were, she had nothing to lose. She'd been ordered to come home, and here she was. If any of Mancuso's people had followed her, they were more skilled than she gave them credit for, but she'd deal with it on the fly if necessary.

She knocked on the door, praying Ryan was inside since she didn't have her keys. A moment later he answered the door, with his hair wet, wearing only a towel, staring at her like she was a ghost. She walked in and placed a finger over her mouth to signal he shouldn't say anything. She figured she was being overly paranoid, but better to play it safe. She motioned for him to get dressed and pointed to the back porch.

While she waited for him to change, she went to the fridge and grabbed two beers. The fridge was full of food, which gave her some sense of comfort since it implied Ryan was feeling at home. She twisted the tops off the beers and walked outside, surprised to see new chairs and a grill in the tiny space. She'd had this apartment for years but had never bothered with more furnishings than a couch, a bed, and a dresser in the entire place. She settled into one of the chairs and took a long pull from her beer. She could get used to this. Her mind wandered to the sunny skies and sandy beaches featured on the website of the resort in Fiji she'd checked out before she'd been roped into taking the Mancuso gig. All she had to do was accept what Wharton was offering—a quick debrief and she could be on her way to a few weeks of nothing but ocean views, unlimited food and drink, and hot women in bikinis sprinkled throughout the landscape. It sounded like paradise until her mind wandered to the memory of Siobhan sans any clothes at all, bringing her coffee in bed yesterday morning. Why would she travel halfway around the world when she could have every creature comfort right here at home?

"Is one of those beers for me?" Ryan walked out onto the patio, pulling the door shut behind him. He'd changed into jeans and a hoodie. "And are we allowed to talk out loud now?"

Royal handed him a beer and clinked her bottle to his. "Yes, but we still need to be careful."

He raised a finger to his lips and nodded. "I guess you can't tell me where you've been."

"I'm not supposed to."

"That's a leading statement."

She took another sip from her beer and contemplated her next step. She wanted his help, but she had no right to ask him to do what she needed unless she was willing to fill him in on the why behind it. It wasn't like she was going to get in more trouble at this point. She downed the rest of her beer, set the bottle on the concrete, reached into her pocket for the burner phone, and handed it to him.

He took it and held it up. "Thanks, sis, but I already have a phone."

"It's my burner phone. The only thing on it is the contents of a flash drive I downloaded."

"Okay. And you're giving it to me because?"

"Because the files are encrypted, and I can't read them."

She knew doling out the information piecemeal wasn't ideal, but she had to work herself up to the big reveal. "The flash drive belonged to the consigliere for the Mancuso family."

Ryan dropped the phone on the table between them like it had stung him. "Holy shit."

"That about sums it up."

"You know, I'm thinking your FBI friends might have people on staff who can read those files."

"They do. The trick is getting them to share what they found with me."

Ryan downed the rest of his beer and set the bottle on the ground beside hers. He stood and left the room, leaving her to wonder what exactly about what she'd said had caused him to leave. She didn't have to wonder too long because less than a minute later, he reappeared with two more beers.

"Look, I know I haven't been real open with you about why I'm home," he said, "but it looks like you have some secrets of your own. Should we clear the air?"

She tilted her beer toward him. "Fine by me. You first."

"I bugged out. Honorable discharge, but I had to fight for it. I turned my CO in for behavior unbecoming, and they tried to trash me. The discharge was a compromise. He stays, I go, and everyone acts like nothing ever happened."

"That's rough." She wanted to ask him for specific details, but then the conversation would devolve into him feeling like he had to justify his decision. The best thing she could do to support him right now was to take it at face value that turning in his CO was the only option he'd had at the time.

"I'm not proud of taking the deal, but it is what it is. I guess I figured I'd die in uniform, but that's done. I'm sure I can find something in security, but after what I've seen and where I've been, I can't wrap my mind around babysitting some pop star or overpaid executive right now. I'm not going to take up permanent residence on your couch, but I need a little more time to figure out my future."

"Take all the time you want, but we're going to have to come up with a schedule for who's doing the cooking because I just got eighty-sixed from the job I was working."

He pointed to the burner phone. "And that's why you need me to hack those files?"

"Yep."

"I promised you I would never use my special talents again."

"I know." When Ryan was a senior in high school, moody and dark, he'd spent hours in his bedroom, dodging their dad between his bouts of sobriety, and earning extra cash by hacking into the school's records to alter grades for other students who were willing to pay. When he leveled up to hacking into the City of Dallas Police Department network to alter arrest records, the feds had shown up at their door. Royal came home from college, cashed in what little savings she had, and hired him a good lawyer, who'd managed to work out a deal. Ryan had walked the local PD through how he'd gotten into their system and he designed a program to keep hackers like him out permanently. In exchange, his case was diverted into a pretrial program and later sealed. The Army had had access to his record, but what had been a potential career killer otherwise only made him more valuable to them as a candidate for special ops.

She picked up the burner phone and stared at the screen while she contemplated her options. He'd promised her he would never again use his skills to commit a crime, and as far as she knew, he hadn't. What she was asking now was definitely in a gray area since she'd been ordered to stand down, but she felt like she was entitled to know what had been on that drive. If it wasn't for her, the bureau wouldn't even have the info and it wasn't like she was stealing it—she was holding it in her hand.

She handed the phone to him. "It's up to you. I doubt anyone will find out we looked at it, but if any trouble comes from it, it's all on me. No one will ever find out you were involved."

"Okay. I'm in." Ryan's eyes gleamed with excitement as he took the phone from her. "I'm going to need an air-gapped computer—one that's never been connected to the internet before, so you're probably going to need to buy one, but before you do that, I need you to think this through. Are you sure you want to see what's on here? You won't be able to unsee it."

It was evidence in a case. What harm could come from looking at it?

Three hours later, they both huddled in front of the laptop she'd acquired at Ryan's direction. They started with the data from the flash drive but, left with more questions than answers, they didn't stop there, and it didn't take long for Royal to realize she couldn't have been more wrong. There was something big happening with the Mancusos, but it wasn't what any of them had expected.

CHAPTER SEVENTEEN

S iobhan was five words into another text to Royal when she hovered over the backspace arrow. If she hit send, this would be the fourth unanswered text since yesterday morning. She'd considered calling Valentino's to see if Royal had shown up for work today, but if Royal dodged her call she didn't need Robert and his crew speculating on their relationship more than they probably already were. Even if Royal was having second thoughts about the intimate side of their relationship, she would've expected her to respond out of respect for her position as consigliere. Either way, she wasn't in the habit of chasing after women, but was she being irrational to think Royal should've texted her back by now?

She didn't know. This was the first time she'd been in this situation—wanting another woman the way she wanted Royal. It was uncomfortable and frustrating and exhilarating and exciting all at once, and she didn't know how to act.

She hit the backspace key, deleted what she'd written so far, and tossed her phone in her desk drawer to keep from being tempted to resume her efforts. Royal would contact her when she was ready, and she'd figure out how to deal with it when she did. In the meantime, she had work to do. She reached into her bag and unzipped the inside pocket. She pulled out the paper with the details about the shell company who owned the SUV that had tried to run her down, but she couldn't find the flash drive she'd stowed there when she'd left the office on Friday.

She checked her computer, but it wasn't there either. She tamped down the rising panic, stuck her hand back in the bag and rummaged around, breathing a sigh of relief when her fingers finally closed around the drive. She placed it in the USB slot on her computer and double-clicked on the desktop icon to open the drive. As usual, a box popped open on the screen asking her to type in her password, but for the first time a warning message greeted her as well.

You have two more chances to enter the correct password.

Siobhan stared at the screen. There had been a couple of times when she'd been working with these reports that she'd accidentally struck a wrong key and received a similar warning when she'd been trying to access the information on the drive, but not like this. The encryption program provided five chances to get the password right. The only way that warning would pop up would be if someone had tried to gain access, used up three tries, and then given up before getting in.

It hadn't been her.

She retraced the entire weekend. She'd placed the flash drive in her bag on Friday before she headed home to get ready for the gala at the museum. She'd fully intended to access the drive on her laptop at home to finish up some reporting over the weekend, but a bomb threat and the meeting with Petrov had intervened.

And Royal. She'd been distracted by Royal. Her calm courage, her gentle affection, and her off-the-charts sexy body had occupied her thoughts both when she was at her side and when she wasn't. Had her distraction allowed someone to access the drive when she wasn't paying attention?

Her bag had only been out of her presence twice that she could recall—while she'd been at the museum Friday night and on Sunday, she'd left it in the car when she and Royal were inside Petrov's compound. The only person who would've had access to her bag on those occasions was Neal. Neal had a key to her apartment, and she had been alone in the car while she and Royal met with Petrov.

She sank back in her chair. The idea Neal might be spying on her was inconceivable. She'd been with the family for years and Carlo had personally selected her to be her driver/bodyguard. She'd trusted her completely when it came to her apartment, her cars, her office. Had Neal betrayed that trust?

There was no way she was going to get any more work done until she had this sorted out. She typed in the password to the flash drive, changed it, made a copy, and locked the copy in her safe, thankful she was the only one with the combination. She placed the original drive back in the zippered pocket of her bag and sent a text to Neal to tell her she was ready to leave for the day. After Neal replied that she would meet her downstairs, she stared at her phone, contemplating her next move. She fully intended to confront Neal, but it would be wise to have backup when she did, and there was only one person she could think of that she wanted to be by her side. She spent a few seconds wavering before she pushed her pride aside and fired off a text to Royal.

I need to talk to you. My place. She glanced at the time, calculating how long it would take her to get home. *Tonight at 7. It's important.*

She pressed send before she could change her mind, grabbed her bag, and went downstairs to meet Neal.

"Did you have a good day?" Neal asked.

She asked the same question every day, but today Siobhan searched her face for some hidden meaning, concerned she'd been missing duplicity on her part all along. "Uneventful, which was a relief. I didn't have any hearings scheduled, which meant I was able to focus on some reports Carlo needs." She paused for a moment to consider how much bait to cast in the water, and then decided to go all in. "I had some trouble accessing one of my password-protected flash drives, which was aggravating."

Neal looked into the rearview mirror and met her eyes. "That's a pain," she said with no particular tone. "Those drives can get corrupted easily, especially if you use them a lot. You should probably switch them out on a regular basis."

"Who knew you were a computer guru?" She smiled to cover her anger that Neal might be a traitor.

"I'm no guru," she said. "Just had a bad experience losing some documents on a drive that stopped working."

"Thanks. Switching them out is good advice." She replayed Neal's words several times in her head and decided she was no closer to determining if she'd been hiding something than she had been before she'd gotten in the car. She decided to wait until she could confront her with Royal before she went any further, and she settled back into silence for the rest of the way home.

A few minutes later, they pulled into the parking garage and she followed Neal into the building. On the elevator ride up, her senses went on high alert as she contemplated whether she'd made the right decision being alone with her like this. What if Royal didn't come? Their complete lack of communication for the past twenty-four hours wasn't a good sign that Royal would drop whatever she was doing and show up to respond to a vague text. She'd wanted to say more. Since Royal had left her bed yesterday, she'd wanted her to come back so she could huddle in the cocoon of affection and passion she felt whenever she was in Royal's presence, but she didn't know how to put into words how she felt or what she wanted from her. All she knew was whatever this was between them, she wanted more of it with a deep and burning desire.

What if Royal didn't show up? Should she confront Neal on her own? What if she did and Neal turned dangerous? She and all the other protection who worked in the Mancuso inner circle were always armed—a fact Siobhan appreciated when it came to her safety, but she'd never before contemplated what would happen if the guns were turned on her. She had a gun of her own, but aside from an occasional visit to the range, it stayed locked in the safe in her closet at home. She didn't even remember if it was loaded.

She waited in the hall while Neal did a walk-through of her apartment, another thing that used to make her feel safe, but now creeped her out as she wondered if she was inside going through her things. When Neal stuck her head out to tell her it was all clear, she was tempted to tell her she could go for the night, unsure she was up for the confrontation to come. She checked her phone one more time, hoping for a text from Royal, but there was nothing and it was time for a choice. She took a deep breath and walked through the door of her apartment, pretending it was the courtroom and she was going to square off with an overzealous prosecutor.

Neal held the door open for her but remained in the doorway. "I'll be in the car if you need me. Pete will take my place in a few hours."

"I could use a drink," Siobhan said. "Are you up for joining me?"

She hesitated, but Siobhan couldn't tell if it was an "I shouldn't drink while on guard duty" or an "I don't want to be subjected to uncomfortable questions" kind of hesitation.

"Are you sure?"

"Absolutely." She strode to the bar and pulled down the bottle of Bow Street. She cradled the bottle for a moment, remembering she'd served it to Royal on their first date. Which hadn't been a date at all, but a demand by her that Royal attend the event at the museum. The "date" had been work for Royal, and maybe that was the problem between them. Every interaction they'd had so far had been cloaked in the guise of a job. How was Royal supposed to know how she really felt when she was sending mixed signals?

But was that really the issue or was it more likely she was the one who was unable to read her own feelings? She didn't have much of a model when it came to relationships. Celia and Tony professed to be in love, but theirs was a lopsided power dynamic where Celia wanted a handsome husband she could boss around, and Tony wanted the cachet that came from being in the Mancuso inner circle. Dominique had a different guy on her arm every week, but she professed none of them meant anything to her. Celia and Dominique's mother had died so long ago, she didn't remember much about her interactions with Carlo, but memory told her their relationship had been stiff and formal, in public anyway.

She wondered if her own mother had been in love with her father. She had very few of her mother's things besides the antique basket she'd shown Royal—her recipes, a heart locket that contained Siobhan's baby picture, and a few scarves— nothing to give her a clue as to whether she'd led a happy life before a stray bullet had cut her life short, suddenly and without warning. Nothing to give her a clue as to who her father had been or whether he had loved her mother and if he had, why he'd never married her.

"Are you okay?"

Neal's voice cut through her reverie. She was here and Siobhan needed to find out if she had betrayed her and she would have to do it alone because solitude was her lot in life. She handed Neal a glass of whiskey, and as she took her first drink, she started her assault with a blunt jab. "Did you copy the flash drive that was in my bag or did you give up when you couldn't figure out the password?"

Neal gulped the whiskey and lowered the glass, wiping her lips with the back of her hand. "What?"

"You heard me." Siobhan took her glass and walked over to the couch. She sat and pointed at the chair across from her. "Put your gun on the table, come over here, and sit down. By the way, I had an extra security camera installed, and it's high-def. If you try anything stupid, Carlo will hunt you down and you will beg for a swift death."

Neal stared at her for a moment with a mixture of what looked like hurt and respect, then made a show of carefully extracting her gun from her shoulder holster and placing it on the table in the entryway where Siobhan usually kept her bag. She walked slowly over to the chair and sat down.

"I don't know what's going on," she said, "but I promise you I don't know what you're talking about."

"Fine. I'll talk, you listen." Siobhan took a sip from her glass, letting the slow burn of the whiskey soothe her nerves. "There was a flash drive in my bag. I specifically remember placing it in the inside zippered pocket on Friday before I left the office. To the casual observer, the drive wouldn't look like much." She reached into her jacket pocket and held it up. "See. Small, gray." She pointed at the label that read *environmental reg research*. "Legal stuff, of limited interest to anyone who wasn't a lawyer. But someone thought it looked interesting enough to take it and try and open the data it contained."

"And you think that was me?"

"I know it was," she bluffed. "The good news is the data is encrypted. If someone tries to log in too many times without success, the information disappears." She spread her fingers wide, letting the drive clatter to the surface of the coffee table between them. "But I suppose you already know that."

Neal leaned forward, her expression desperate. "I promise you I don't." She held her palms up. "I don't know anything about a flash drive or your reports. I may have—" She stopped abruptly and frowned.

"You may have what?" Siobhan asked, growing impatient with this exercise.

"Wait, you said the flash drive was in your bag?" She pointed to the table where her gun lay next to Siobhan's bag. "Was your bag where it is now?"

"Neal, I'm not playing around. I've made a call and if you don't come clean with me, someone else is going to get you to talk and it won't be over a nice glass of whiskey." She hoped her poker face was still working.

"It was Royal."

Hearing Royal's name when she'd been wishing she was here jarred Siobhan and she had to scramble to stay calm. "What are you talking about?"

"Sunday, after the meeting with Petrov. She came home with you. You were in your room and she was helping me check the rest of the apartment out. I found her with her hand in your bag. What other reason would she have for going through your bag unless she was taking the drive or putting it back? I practically caught her in the act and she made up some bullshit about how she was checking the plug for the lamp."

She took a breath and started to say more, but Siobhan cut her off. "Be quiet." Neal was talking too fast for her to process and she wasn't making sense.

Or was she? She'd brought the drive home on Friday. Royal had stayed over. They'd made love —make that had sex—until late into the night. She closed her eyes and pictured Royal sitting on the side of her bed pulling on her clothes. She hadn't walked her to the door. Instead she'd rolled over and pretended to go back to sleep, not wanting to admit or display her disappointment Royal wasn't staying the night. Royal could've taken the drive on her way out and returned it on Sunday. Okay, so the opportunity was there, but could Royal really be that duplicitous without her having a clue?

She had the drive back now and Royal was MIA. Was that a coincidence or a sign she'd been naive to trust her in the first place? Had she been too quick to bring Royal into the family without the kind of vetting a stranger would normally get?

She saved your life.

It was true. Royal had saved her. The day the SUV tried to mow her down, but even more than that, she'd saved her from a loneliness she'd felt her entire life, even before she'd become an orphan and the pseudo stepsister to the Mancuso sisters. Royal had given her hope that she could find happiness. Had it all been an illusion?

Her phone buzzed and she opened her eyes. Neal was still sitting across from her, her eyes laced with concern. She'd had ample opportunity during her little foray into self-pity to grab her gun and leave, but she hadn't. While she processed exactly what that meant, she picked up her phone and stared at the alert telling her she had an incoming text from an unknown number. Strangely compelled, she opened the text and stared at the message.

It's R. I'm on my way up. I have something important to tell you. Please wait for me.

CHAPTER EIGHTEEN

Since when did you start driving like a little old lady?" Royal said, pointing at the speedometer. "The speed limit through here is fifty."

Ryan accelerated through the next intersection. "I thought the goal was to get you there alive. Besides, do you really want to risk getting pulled over right now? I'll get us there. Try and relax."

Royal took a deep breath. Technically, she was on the run, having disobeyed a direct order from Wharton. She hadn't reported in, she'd ignored his calls, and she'd moved to a hotel under an assumed name while she figured out her next step. Ryan was right. Getting pulled over would create even more problems, but his advice didn't do much to quell the rising anxiety she had about getting to Siobhan as quickly as possible. She and Ryan had spent the past twenty-four hours sorting out what was real and what wasn't when it came to the Mancuso family empire, a deep dive that had taken them into the FBI's internal servers, well beyond what she was cleared to see. After everything she'd seen she was convinced Siobhan was in trouble and the threat was closer than any of them had realized.

Ryan had managed to hack into the contents of the flash drive she'd saved to her burner phone. It was full of information about the structure of the Mancuso operation that would be useful to law enforcement, but it was what he didn't find that had triggered them to go further. She'd almost become lost in the process and had nearly missed Siobhan's last text. But it had come in moments after she and Ryan had discovered pivotal information, and she'd typed a quick reply and hoped she wasn't too late. She closed her eyes and replayed the last twenty-four hours.

"There's more here, but the files are corrupted. It could've happened during the transfer."

Royal cursed the fact she no longer had the drive. She couldn't articulate why it was imperative that she see what was on it, but she knew it was.

"What do you want to do?" Ryan asked, his fingers poised over the laptop she'd purchased.

"If the file is corrupted on the phone, does that mean it's corrupted everywhere?" she asked.

"Not necessarily." He cracked his knuckles and pointed at the screen. "But there's no way to know for sure unless we look at the other copy. I think I can do it, if that's what you want."

She choked back a laugh. What she wanted was to have never agreed to this assignment in the first place. If she'd simply said no, she'd be on a beach somewhere and some other agent would be tasked with figuring out what to do about the Mancuso family. If she'd said no, she wouldn't be conflicted about how her feelings for Siobhan were interfering with her duty. Or would she? She liked to think she'd have issues with the way she'd been yanked off this case whether or not she cared how Siobhan might be affected. After all, she'd taken Siobhan's flash drive even while she was falling for her.

She replayed the thought in her head, recognizing her feelings for Siobhan were the ultimate issue. She'd worked deep undercover numerous times throughout her career, but never once had she been swept away by an attraction that was supposed to be pretend. She'd never had to pretend with Siobhan, not about how she felt anyway. From the moment she'd met Siobhan on the street downtown, she'd been intrigued, and she wasn't sure she would have agreed to this assignment if Siobhan hadn't been part of the allure. She'd compromised her principles in exchange for feeling alive and desired, and if she told Ryan to keep going—to hack into the FBI servers—she would go from taking a few steps down the path of her curiosity to running full out into a fire that might kill her career.

But what was her career worth if she couldn't trust the integrity of those who commanded her, and right now she was certain something wasn't right. She'd been ripped from the Garza case and now she'd been ripped from this one. Wharton had called her repeatedly in the past day, but she'd chosen to ignore him since he would only tell her to get her ass into HQ for the debrief, but she wasn't ready to share what she knew when he wasn't willing to share back. Wharton would find her eventually, but she had the resources and skill to be able to evade him until she got some answers, starting with what else was on that drive.

"Do it," she said. Ryan started typing right away. She hated involving him, but she didn't know who else she could trust. For the next hour, she paced while he typed.

"I'm in," he called out, clasping his hands above his head in victory.

Royal stopped pacing and practically dove across the room to join him in front of the laptop. "Show me."

He pointed at the screen. "Here is the rest of the contents of the flash drive. Mostly spreadsheets, showing cash flow between the various Mancuso businesses." He pointed at a line of code. "The spreadsheet was generated by someone named D. Mancuso."

"That would be Dominique. Carlo's oldest daughter. She keeps the books."

"Okay, well, apparently she's a creative accountant, because look here." He pointed at a split screen. "I ran a search for her name on the server and turned up this chart. See, the chart has different numbers than the spreadsheet from the drive, and those," he pointed to a row of seemingly random numbers, "those are offshore account numbers. It looks like there have been large transfers to other organizations and accounts, not on the list of Mancuso holdings."

"Can you tell who made the transfers?"

"I'm not a magician." He grinned. "But I can read." He entered a few more keystrokes, and a 302, the standard FBI form for memorializing investigative notes, filled the screen. "Looks like the forensic team at FBI HQ already ran down the lead."

Royal skimmed the document. The overseas accounts had been traced back to Dominique Mancuso. She stopped reading. "That doesn't tell us anything we don't already know. It's not unusual for organized crime families to have some of the holdings in offshore accounts."

"Could she be skimming from the family till?" He put both charts up on the screen. "The numbers from the spreadsheet that came from the flash drive list total holdings for the various businesses, but the totals on the chart from the

FBI server don't match. Maybe Dominique was engaged in creative accounting."

"I guess so, but I'm not sure I can figure it out from what we have here." Her mind started churning, but every path for a possible solution led back to Siobhan. Should she take this information to her? She'd be breaking every rule in the book if she did, but she had a gut feeling there was some connection between what her boss wasn't telling her, what Ryan had found, and the threat against the Mancuso family in general and Siobhan in particular. "Are there any other 302s that mention any of the Mancusos or..." She thought for a second and then decided to give her hunch a stab. "Or Mikhail Petrov?"

"Got it." His fingers flew over the keyboard. "We shouldn't stay in much longer or we might get caught."

"Will they be able to trace us here?"

"Not right away. I'm piggybacking over a different IP address, but it's not a permanent solution."

She stared at the various screens flying by, unable to keep up. "You're really good at this."

He grinned again. "It's a calling. Or, as Dad said when I was arrested, a curse. The Army didn't seem to mind using me to do their bidding."

"You don't have to do this for me," she said, catching the bitterness behind his words. "I'm sorry for putting you in this position."

"You're the only person who's ever looked out for me," he said. "I'd do anything for you."

She threw an arm around his shoulder and pulled him close. "Right back at you."

"Hey, I think I found something."

She stared at the screen and drank in the words, certain

she now had a handle on who was behind the threat against the Mancuso family. "Can you screenshot that? All of it."

She stood and reached for her gun and her jacket, but hesitated about her badge, ultimately deciding it might help to have it. Besides, she was done pretending. "I have to go take care of something."

"Right now?"

"Yes. If I don't come back, send this information to that investigative reporter for the Dallas Morning News. *Ellis Pearson."*

He closed the laptop. "I'll do you one better. I'm coming with you."

"This is her building." Royal pointed. "Up here on the right. Drop me at the curb and grab a space on the street because the only other options are a gated parking garage or the valet."

"I'll park on the street, but I'm coming with you."

She considered taking him up on it but decided this was something she had to do alone. "I may need to get away fast and it'll be better if you're here and ready to go."

"Okay, but tell me one thing."

"Name it."

"Why are you doing this? The FBI is your life. No judgment here, but whatever you're up to, you could be throwing it all away."

She stood at the car window and considered his question. It was a fair ask and she could think of a bunch of complicated, convoluted answers as to why she felt compelled to keep working a case after she'd been ordered to stop—duty, justice, a desire to get to the truth—but none of those things explained why she would be willing to ditch her career. What really hung in the balance was her loyalty and who deserved it more—the agency who'd been jerking her around or the woman who'd awoken feelings she thought she'd never have. What they'd found in the belly of the FBI server confirmed her suspicions that, without her knowledge, the agency had been using her for more than she'd signed on to do, and her decision about what to do with that realization all boiled down to one thing. "I guess I realized I need a life beyond the bureau, and the only person who's going to make that happen is me."

He held up his hand in salute. "Go. Do what you need to do and I'll be right here waiting."

The elevator ride took forever, but it gave her time to gather her thoughts. She had no idea what she was walking into, but after being radio silent with Siobhan for the last twenty-four hours, she expected her to be pissed. Had she summoned her here out of affection or anger? Royal didn't care as long as she was okay. Now, she just had to get Siobhan to listen to what she had to say.

When the elevator finally stopped on the penthouse floor, she lunged out the doors and rapped her knuckles on Siobhan's door. "It's me, Royal." She didn't have to wait long before the door swung open, but instead of Siobhan, Neal was standing in the doorway with a gun in her hand.

"What's the matter?" Royal asked, stepping into Neal's space. "Is Siobhan okay?"

Neal reached for her shoulder and pushed her back. "Hold up. Are you carrying?"

"Yes, and you better answer my question right now or you're going to see it up close."

"You talk tough for someone who doesn't have the advantage here." Neal pointed her gun at her chest. "She's inside and she's fine. Put your weapon on the floor, nice and easy, then I might let you see her."

She didn't have a choice if she wanted to get by her unless

she wanted to risk a shootout, which would only bring the cops, which would only invite questions. Taking some comfort from Neal's promise that Siobhan was okay, she eased her gun out of her holster and set it carefully on the ground. "She asked me to come over. Are you going to take me to her or what?"

Neal motioned for her to walk ahead of her into the apartment and shut the door behind them. Siobhan was sitting on the couch in the living room, but she was staring at something in her hand and didn't look up as they approached. Neal shoved her into a chair and stood, looming behind her in true bodyguard fashion. Royal sat in the ominous quiet for what felt like forever until she was no longer able to handle the silence.

"Siobhan, you asked me to come and I'm here."

Siobhan slowly raised her head and Royal could see the hurt in her eyes, and she knew she was partly responsible for the pain, and on track to deliver more.

"Did you take this from me?"

Royal stared at the flash drive in Siobhan's hand. There was no point lying now. "Yes."

"Why?"

Here it was. Whatever she said next would define their relationship forever. A lie and she'd never be able to come clean, but she might never recover from telling the truth since it would cast doubt on everything that had gone before. There was only one clear choice, and she'd have to accept whatever consequences followed.

"My real name is Royal Scott and I'm a special agent for the FBI."

CHAPTER NINETEEN

Siobhan wanted to ask Royal to repeat what she'd said but feared it might be even worse to hear it for a second time. She glanced at Neal, who was still standing behind Royal, her gun at the ready. One word from her and the threat against her family would be eliminated, and if Royal were anyone else, she wouldn't have hesitated.

But she'd trusted this woman, invited her into her life and made love to her. She'd allowed herself to imagine a relationship, a family of her own.

Pipe dreams. More proof such longings were the stuff of fantasy, and she felt silly now for having entertained the notion she wasn't better off on her own.

"You're an undercover agent?" she asked.

"Yes. I was assigned to infiltrate the organization and learn everything I could about your current business practices and gather intel on any new operations going down."

Royal stared straight at her as she spoke, and the sustained contact was disconcerting. How many times had she stared into those eyes, wondering what Royal was thinking about her. Now she had her answer. Royal had been thinking about her as a target, her only goal to figure out a way to take them all down. She held up the flash drive. "Did you manage to see what was on here?"

"Yes. The bureau has everything that's on there."

More disconcerting than Royal's stare was the frank honesty of her admissions. "And you figured you'd come to tell me this because you're a stand-up person who doesn't like to keep secrets?"

Royal's jaw clenched and she glanced back at Neal.

"You can speak freely in front of her. I trust *her*."

Royal flinched slightly at the emphasis. Siobhan thought it would make her feel better to see Royal in pain, but it only made her sad. "Tell me why you came."

"I came to warn you. Dominique is up to something with the family business."

"That's it? You come here, announce you work for the FBI, and tell me Dominique Mancuso is up to something with her own damn business?"

"She's running a side business with Petrov. They are both playing Carlo, trying to squeeze him out, and I can prove it."

Dread curled around Siobhan's spine. What Royal was saying sounded crazy. It was the kind of thing federal agents said to coax admissions and confessions, but this type of strategy was usually employed in interrogation rooms when the target was vulnerable. They were in her house, her safe space, and Royal, gun to her back, was the one who was vulnerable. She could be lying to try to get out of a difficult situation, but then again, she hadn't had to come here in the first place. "Say it again."

"Dominique has aligned with Petrov. She doesn't agree with her father's decision to stay out of prostitution and drugs to grow the Mancuso empire, so she's been reaching out to new contacts. In addition to Petrov, she's made overtures to the Garza cartel. I have a copy of the file documenting all of this on my phone. It's in the left front pocket of my jacket."

"She could fake documents," Neal said, her first contribution to the conversation.

"I could, but I didn't. The documents contain information about numbered accounts where Dominique has been sending money she'd siphoned off from the main business. Feel free to check it out."

Siobhan looked at Neal and nodded. She leaned over and roughly pushed aside Royal's jacket, yanking a phone from the inside pocket, which she handed over. Siobhan held it up and looked at the screen.

"What you're looking for is in a folder labeled Flynn," Royal said.

"How original." Siobhan stood. "I'll be right back." The walk to her home office took forever, but when she was finally behind the closed door, she allowed herself to breathe. She paced in front of her desk, trying to drain the adrenaline that had been building the entire time Royal had been spinning her fantastical tale.

But what if she was telling the truth?

Siobhan sat at her desk and started scrolling through the documents on Royal's phone. The first one was the spreadsheet of accounts that had been on the flash drive Royal had taken from her. She studied it for a moment, but the document didn't appear to have been altered in any way. She flicked it away and went on to the next. It was another chart of accounts, but she'd never seen this one before. The categories for the accounts were the same, but this one had different account numbers, numbers she didn't recognize. She scrolled through a few other pages of spreadsheets that didn't make sense to her out of context, and then she reached a 302. She recognized the form—she'd received plenty of 302 forms during her representation of clients in federal court, but she'd never seen one with her name on it.

Witness states that Siobhan Collins is the consigliere to Carlo Mancuso. She is widely believed to be his pick to take over the family business, which is why Dominique Mancuso, Carlo's older daughter, has been aligning her interests with other parties, including Mikhail Petrov.

There was more detail, but it all amounted to the same thing—someone had told the FBI Dominique had betrayed her own family, and the FBI had documented evidence to back up the claim.

She looked at the top of the form. She didn't recognize the interviewing agent's name, and all it said in the space for the name of the witness who'd provided the FBI with this salacious gossip was CI-1. Confidential information number one. So, there were two traitors in their midst, Royal and whoever else the FBI had turned against them. And if this evidence was real, Dominique was the biggest traitor of all.

She drummed her fingers on her desk, running through options. She needed to act, but she couldn't make a move on a family member without verifying that this intel was correct. Who did she know that could get inside information that wouldn't be traced back to her?

No sooner had she formed the question than she knew exactly who to call. She reached for her phone, scrolled through her contacts until she came to the Ms, and pressed the button for the first entry. She rarely used this number—too rarely—and she hoped her old friend would be receptive to her request.

"Yes?" The voice was cautious, but familiar.

"Muriel, it's Shiv."

"Shiv, it's been too long. How are you?"

"I've been better. I know it's been too long since I reached out, and I'm ashamed to say I'm calling you because I need your help."

"Time and distance is nothing between friends, Shiv. Tell me what I can do for you?"

Siobhan started tearing up at the gentle, friendly tone of Muriel's voice. During law school at Tulane, she and Muriel Casey had been fast friends, but after graduation, she'd returned to Texas and Muriel had stayed in New Orleans to join her cousin Cain's operation. For the first few years, they'd stayed in contact, but over time they'd lost touch. She'd seen Muriel briefly months ago when she'd been in New Orleans to handle a case before the Fifth Circuit. She'd joined Muriel and her girlfriend, Kristen, for dinner along with Cain and her wife, Emma, and the memory of their tight-knit family had stuck with her to this day. Muriel was probably the closest thing she'd ever had to a sister and she'd been foolish to let their connection fade.

"Are you okay?"

Muriel's voice was laced with concern which only caused Siobhan to tear up more. "No, but I hope to be soon."

"Speak freely, my friend. This is a secure line and I trust you can say the same for your end."

Siobhan blurted out the whole story. All about Royal and how she'd fallen for her charm and invited her into the family's inner circle only to find out she was the enemy. And Dominique, and how her constant barbs about how Carlo was running the family business had turned into actual betrayal.

"And Carlo is sick. He has cancer. He's been hiding it as best he can, but Dominique knows, which is probably why she's been more aggressive lately. If what the FBI has on her is to be believed, she has been secretly moving money so she can invest in other interests—drugs, prostitution—things Carlo would never approve."

"Tell me what you need."

"I need to know if what Royal is saying is true. I have what appear to be FBI files and her word, but I don't know if I can trust either. I have contacts here, but I can't use them because I don't know who to trust. I was hoping you or Cain might be able to find a way to verify these claims. I can't make a move unless I know I'm on solid ground."

"You know there was a time, not that long ago, when a certain FBI agent caught my heart."

"And broke it, if I recall," Siobhan said. "See, no good can come of this."

"Good can come from the strangest places," Muriel said. "Just because it didn't work for me doesn't mean you're in the same boat. Shelby's betrayal was a stab to my heart mostly because it came after I'd fallen for her, but it sounds like your agent friend lied to you in the beginning but is trying to make up for her deception now that she has feelings for you. Completely different situation. I only bring up Shelby to say that I'm probably not the best person to find a source within the bureau to confirm what you've been told, but Shelby does owe Cain a favor. More than one. Perhaps we can work something out. Send me what you have, and I'll do what I can."

"Thank you. I'll be ready to repay the favor."

Siobhan forwarded the documents to Muriel as soon as she hung up the phone. That done, she stared at the door to her study and wished she had a secret exit so she could escape without having to face Royal until she knew what was in store for them next. She knew she should be focused on the business consequences of Dominique's actions, but she was still digesting what Muriel had said about Royal.

Royal could've very easily made up a lie about the flash drive, and she would've believed her because she didn't want to think she'd been falling for someone who would betray her trust. Instead, Royal had shown up here without being forced or threatened to do so, and she'd confessed her role in trying to take down the family business. What was her angle? Royal couldn't be naive enough to think an aw-shucks routine would have Siobhan holding out her hands, asking to be arrested? Royal had handed over what appeared to be classified FBI files without asking for anything in return. Was Muriel's implication right? Did that mean Royal had feelings for her, and if so, what was she going to do about it?

A knock on the door startled her out of her thoughts. "Come in," she called out, too overwhelmed to care who she was inviting in.

Neal stuck her head through the door, her face red and her expression flustered. "What is it?" Siobhan asked, dreading the answer.

"It's Don Carlo. He collapsed. Michael took him to the hospital, but he's in bad shape."

She gripped the edge of the desk. "Who else knows?"

"Celia and Tony aren't due back from Venice until next week, and Michael hasn't been able to reach Dominique."

"Tell him to quit trying for now. Tell him I want extra security on the don's room, around the clock." She grabbed her phone and the one Royal had given her off of her desk. "Let's go." She said a silent prayer as she walked through the house while simultaneously making a mental checklist of things she needed to do. When she reached the living room, thing number one was still seated in the chair where she'd left her, but she rose as Siobhan approached.

"Are you okay?" Royal asked, her voice laced with concern. "I heard. Carlo is tough. He's going to be okay."

"You don't know that," Siobhan snapped. "You don't know him at all."

"You're right, but I do know how important he is to you." Royal reached for her hand. "I have a car waiting out front and my badge will get you through the hospital red tape. Please, let me do this for you."

Siobhan stared into her kind and caring eyes. Royal said all the right things, did all the right things. Why did the one woman who'd captured her heart have to be her adversary as well?

CHAPTER TWENTY

Royal held Siobhan's hand as they raced out of her building, determined not to let go for fear Siobhan would make a break for it. She needn't have worried. Siobhan, who'd seemed laser-focused back in her apartment, had fallen into a haze when Royal had taken charge, and Royal wondered if she ever had a break from having to be on, always ready to handle whatever crisis might arise.

"It's up here," she said, leading Siobhan to the sidewalk in front of her building and toward the boxy white rental car, acutely conscious of Neal right on their heels. She'd texted Ryan from the elevator and told him to have the engine running, hoping he wouldn't be fazed when she showed up with Siobhan and her bodyguard in tow. She opened the rear passenger door and helped Siobhan in and slid into the seat beside her, never letting go of her hand.

"Where are we headed?" Ryan asked, with a wary glance at Neal who'd slipped into the front passenger seat.

"Presbyterian Hospital." Royal waited until they were on the expressway, and then she made introductions. "Ryan, this is Siobhan and her bodyguard, Neal."

"Are you FBI too?" Siobhan asked Ryan.

He laughed. "Not in a million years. Retired Army special ops with a specialty in computer operations."

"Sounds fancy."

"It was. I got paid to use a lot of high-tech weapons and was given permission to hack into other people's computers, but it wasn't all it was cracked up to be." He smiled at Royal. "Is this your life beyond the bureau?"

She waved her hand in front of her throat, hoping he'd get the hint and shut up, but Siobhan intervened. "What's that supposed to mean?" she asked.

"Uh…" Ryan looked back at Royal, who shook her head in defeat. "Nothing. We were talking earlier about leaving jobs we no longer found fulfilling."

"Is that so?"

"Truth. I think my big sister is ready to make the leap."

Royal wanted to find a way to tell him to shut up without Siobhan noticing, especially since she was getting death glares from Neal, but Ryan's banter seemed to be providing a welcome distraction for the ride to the hospital and whatever awaited Siobhan there. She looked down at their still joined hands and caught Siobhan looking as well. "Is this okay?"

Siobhan sighed. "I don't know. I can't think about it right now. Please don't make me think about it right now."

"Absolutely. Whatever you need."

Siobhan closed her eyes, and they spent the rest of the ride in silence. At one point during the drive, Royal caught Ryan watching them in the rearview mirror, and he mouthed, "good for you," to her and she'd smiled in return. It was true. The exhilaration she got from being with Siobhan was so much better than the fake high she got from risking her life for a job that had used her for years only to shut her out without notice or a plausible explanation. Siobhan might never forgive her for the lies she'd told, but she wasn't ready to give up yet.

When they pulled up to the hospital, Royal gently nudged Siobhan and whispered, "We're here."

"I'll find a place to park," Ryan said.

"Thanks. I'll text you when I know where things stand." Royal helped Siobhan out of the car and led her to the emergency room with Neal close behind. She walked past the waiting line of patients and flashed her badge at the nurse at the desk. "I need to see Carlo Mancuso. He came in about an hour ago."

The badge did the trick, and seconds later, Nurse Randall led the three of them to a private ICU room. She pointed at Michael who was standing in front of the door. "You'll have to figure out how to get past this guy on your own. He hasn't moved since they got here."

Royal thanked the nurse and she took off back to her station. Siobhan hugged Michael and asked about Carlo. "What happened?"

"He didn't eat all day. Said he wasn't hungry, but I could tell he was feeling bad. Sal brought some broth to his room for dinner, and he didn't answer the door. He walked in and found him on the floor. Don't know how long he'd been out. I figured I could get him here faster than an ambulance. He's been asking for you."

"Any word from Dominique?"

"No, and I stopped trying to reach her after I talked to you." He jerked his chin toward the door. "He hasn't asked."

"Good. No one gets in here without my say-so."

"Understood. He'll be glad to see you."

Neal placed her hand on Siobhan's shoulder. "Do you want me to come with you?" she asked.

Royal spotted the concern in Neal's eyes and knew she was as worried about Siobhan as she was about Carlo, but although she had no right to expect an invitation so soon after Siobhan discovered she was an agent and not an ally, *she* wanted to be the one by Siobhan's side when she stepped inside that room. Thankfully, Siobhan's next words laid her doubt to rest.

"I need you to stay with Michael and guard this door as if your lives depend on it." Siobhan turned to Royal. "Come with me."

She'd phrased it like a command, but Royal recognized it as a plea, and she was ready to step up. When she'd told Siobhan she'd give her whatever she needed, she'd meant it. She had a lot to prove, and she'd start right now by supporting Siobhan in whatever way she needed.

❖

Siobhan gasped when they entered the room. She'd expected Carlo's condition to be dire, but she wasn't prepared for the crowded array of machines and tangle of tubes and wires covering his frail body. She dropped Royal's hand and grasped the rail of Carlo's bed.

"You made it."

His voice was weak and raspy, but she was overjoyed to hear him speak at all. "Of course. Someone has to make sure they take good care of you."

"I need to tell you something," he croaked. "Something important."

"Whatever you have to say, it can wait. Let's work on getting you healthy again." She reached for the blanket and pulled it up around his shoulders. She started to pull back, but he caught her hand in his and gripped hard.

"Grant a dying man his last wish."

He wasn't dying. He couldn't be. She stared into his eyes and willed it not to be so, but she knew better. A month ago, she would've thought he'd be with them for a few more years, but since the wedding, she'd noticed a decline. Had he held out to see Celia married, and now he was ready for some permanent rest? Or had the stress of their recent troubles taken their toll on his health? It didn't matter now. He was dying and all she could do was give him whatever he needed in his final moments. She clasped his hand in both of hers. "I'm here."

He raised his other hand and pointed at Royal. "Do you want me to ask her to leave?" Siobhan asked.

"No, she should hear this too."

Siobhan motioned for Royal to join them and she walked over and stood close. Carlo motioned for Royal to bend closer to him and he whispered something in her ear. Royal nodded at his words, her expression serious.

"Promise," he said, loud enough for Siobhan to hear.

"I promise," Royal replied.

Siobhan raised her eyebrows in question, but Royal shook her head and she supposed she'd have to wait to find out what had just transpired. She turned her attention back to Carlo and said in a teasing tone, "I thought you wanted to tell *me* something."

"I never told you exactly how your mother died. You were so young. All these years I thought I was protecting you, but I know now I robbed you of your heritage."

She shook her head. "It doesn't matter. You gave me a good life. You could've sent me off to a home or foster care when she died. I will always be thankful for your kindness."

He sighed. "It wasn't a kindness. I loved you from the moment you were born. You had her eyes, her smile. You were perfect in every way and it killed me to deny you. You, my firstborn child."

He erupted into a coughing fit, and Siobhan stood stock-still unsure she'd heard him correctly. Had he just said...Had he called her his child? The room started to swim, and she gripped the bedrail like it was a life preserver, keeping her safe against the crashing waves of his declaration. She felt strong arms encircle her from behind, and she leaned back into Royal's embrace. After a moment, she felt steady again, and Carlo's coughs subsided enough for him to keep going.

"We were going to run away together, but the day before we were to leave, Sophia came to me and said she was pregnant with Dominique. I was young and ambitious. I chose to stay with my wife because it was easier, because it was what was expected, but I only ever loved your mother. She stayed on at the house and settled for the small pieces of time I was able to steal away from the life I'd chosen. The day she died? That bullet was meant for me. If she hadn't stayed with me, given up a chance at a full life, she might be alive right now. I have robbed you of two parents, and I will go to my grave with regret because of it."

She had questions. Tons of them. Details, specifics. Her lawyer mind listed them, point by point. Had Sophia Mancuso known? Had Dominique? Who else knew? Why was he telling her this now? She got that he wanted to let this secret go before he died, but why burden her with this truth when she'd made peace with the lie long ago?

But he was dying, and to interrogate him now seemed cruel and unnecessary. She'd always loved him like a father. No reason to erase that now that it was official. She bent down and kissed him on the forehead. "I love you. No regrets."

She started to straighten back up, but he reached for her arm and held her in place. "You didn't choose this life. You've made it work, but it's not for you. It wasn't for your mother either. I don't know what I could've become if I'd chosen to be with her, but I think I would've been happy. You have a chance to be happy. I've made sure you'll never want for money. Leave this life." He gasped, and his last words were a whisper. "Be with the one you love."

She stood perfectly still, bent over his chest, waiting for more. Words, sounds, anything to signal he was still with them, even though she knew in her heart he was gone. The machine closest to them rang a flat, steady tone to make it official, and she clutched him in her arms in the kind of over-the-top show of affection they'd both always avoided.

She had no idea how long she'd been holding him when Royal eased her away. The machines were silent now and two nurses were in the room, almost done gently extracting him from the web of wires and tubes. She stared at his face, as peaceful as she'd ever seen it. He'd lived for years with a burdensome secret, but now he was free, and the burden was hers to carry. She had a father, or rather she'd had a father, and he'd loved her deeply. That would have to be enough for now.

"Siobhan."

She turned into Royal's arms. "I know. We need to go, but I need to speak to Michael before we leave."

With one last look at Carlo, she left the room with Royal. Michael was standing guard still, and she told Royal she'd be right back. She pulled Michael aside and broke the news. He took it quietly, but he'd been with Carlo for years and she knew he had to be taking it almost as hard as she was. There was work to do, though, and she gave him instructions on the funeral arrangements. The preparations had been made a year ago when his diagnosis had first become dire. Normally, a don of his stature would warrant a large service with family and friends at the church and graveside, followed by gatherings well into the night, but he'd left very specific instructions about the disposition of his remains. He was to be cremated and his ashes buried in the family plot. He didn't forbid a service, but he didn't want one. She hadn't understood the reasoning behind his requests when he'd first shared them with her, but his revelations made it more clear. The people who would show up to celebrate his life hadn't really known him at all, and he'd rather go quietly than with fanfare he didn't feel he deserved.

Michael assured her he would set Carlo's plan in motion, and she returned to Royal's side.

"I just heard something buzz. Your phone, maybe?" Royal said, handing over her purse.

She'd forgotten she'd asked Royal to hang on to it while she spoke with Carlo. She reached into the bag and pulled out the phone. She didn't recognize the number for the missed call, but she had a text from Muriel. *Be on the lookout for an important call.* She'd barely finished reading it when the phone rang again. "Hello?"

"Siobhan, it's your good friend's cousin."

It had been years, but she instantly recognized the easy cadence of Cain Casey's voice. She grasped Royal's hand and ducked into an empty room. She held the phone between them so Royal could hear too. "It's good to hear from you."

"I'm sorry for your loss, lass. He was a good man."

She didn't bother asking how Cain knew Carlo was dead. Cain Casey had a multitude of contacts and knew everything that happened in the south and beyond. "Thank you. I don't know what I'm going to do without him."

"I'm afraid you're going to have to find out, and quickly. Those documents you sent check out. She's transferred the bulk of his fortune and business interests into accounts under her name, though some are co-owned by that Russian asshole."

Damn. Thank God Carlo wasn't around to witness the extent of his daughter's betrayal. "Any suggestions?"

"The way I see it, you have two choices. You can fight her for control, or you can walk away and start your own empire someplace else. I highly recommend somewhere without an extradition treaty. Either way, I'd stake you in a heartbeat."

"Thank you, but I've planned well for my future. I don't think I have it in me to fight right now. Feel free to make a move on anything that's left."

"Understood. If you change your mind, the offer stands. Oh, and your sweetheart, the fed? She's been burned. If she still has a badge, it won't be good much longer and her passport will be flagged as well. If you need help in that regard, you let Muriel know and she'll take care of you."

"I appreciate the offer, but I know some people."

"I bet you do. You're going to be just fine, but if you ever need anything, you let us know."

Cain was right. In time, she would be fine, but if she was going to run, there were people she'd have to leave behind. "There is one thing. Two loyal employees will need a safe place to land. I hate to ask for more of your generosity, but if there's anything you can do—"

"Send Muriel the details and consider it done. Loyalty should always be rewarded. Now, go and be safe. We'll talk again when you're ready to make a move."

Siobhan thanked her and clicked off the line. She sent a quick text to Muriel with Michael and Neal's contact info, comforted to know they would be safe from any revenge Dominique might choose to exact. When she was done, she turned to Royal. Despite the news that the people she'd worked with for her entire adult life had just tossed her aside like garbage, Royal was as calm and steady and confident as the first day they'd met, and Siobhan couldn't think of anyone she'd rather have by her side today or any day. She pulled Royal close and kissed her. Lightly, but with the promise of more to come. "Okay, sweetheart. What do we do now?"

CHAPTER TWENTY-ONE

Royal reached for the remote and pressed the button for the blinds. A whisper quiet whirring sounded, and bright sunshine filled the room. Beside her, Siobhan covered her face with a pillow.

"It burns. It burns."

"It does not." Royal took advantage of the fact Siobhan was holding the pillow with both hands to tickle her ribs which, in turn, started a faux wrestling match. Within moments, Siobhan was straddling her waist. She stretched her naked body over Royal's and pinned her wrists above her head.

"What did I tell you about tickling?"

Royal laughed. "All I know is I'm pretty happy with how this bout ended."

She leaned up and took Siobhan's breast in her mouth, tracing circles around her nipple with her tongue. Siobhan moaned against the touch, and within moments, she was rocking in place, her clit hard and wet against Royal's skin. Royal placed a hand on either side of Siobhan's waist and continued licking and teasing and sucking her breasts. Within moments, Siobhan stiffened in her arms and cried out before collapsing at her side. She curled around her, huddled close, and whispered in her ear, "How do you do that? Every. Single. Time."

"What?"

"Have an orgasm within thirty seconds of waking up."

A slow smile spread across Siobhan's face. "Uh, I had a little help." She turned so they were facing and traced a finger down Royal's chest. "Let's see if we can set a new record, but this time it's your turn."

A knock on the door startled them both. Siobhan placed a finger over Royal's lips. "Housekeeping. If we're very quiet, maybe they'll go away."

"Are you two awake yet? The boat leaves in thirty minutes. I brought coffee."

Royal groaned at the sound of Ryan's voice. "The reef tour. I totally forgot."

Siobhan sat up. "I'd say let's skip, but he's been looking forward to it, and we kind of owe him."

"Because he hacked into Dominique's accounts and transferred all the money to us? Trust me, his cut was more than enough to make up for many, many missed reef tours."

Siobhan swung her legs over the side of the bed and pulled Royal with her. "Be nice. He's the only family we have. Besides, he brought coffee." She tossed a shirt at Royal. "Put this on. I'll get the door."

Royal pulled on the shirt, fished around in the bed until she found a pair of boxers, and then joined Siobhan and Ryan in the kitchen of their bungalow. The ocean view from this room was as spectacular as the bedroom.

"Here's your coffee." Siobhan handed her a mug and pointed out the window. "Are you ever going to get tired of the view?"

"I don't think so. I'd sleep with the blinds up if you'd let me."

"You two should buy a place here," Ryan chimed in. "Seriously. You can afford it, and at some point it's going to get old living in a hotel. Even one as nice as this."

Royal looked at Siobhan to gauge her interest. They'd chosen Maldives as their first stop on the run from the feds tour because it fit two major criteria—no extradition treaty with the US and the spectacular beaches she craved—but when it came to settling down together, they hadn't discussed doing it at all, let alone where they'd end up. She assumed they'd get to that at some point, but up until now she'd been content to enjoy the simplicity of sea, sand, and solitude with Siobhan at her side.

The rest of the day, Ryan's words echoed in her head. There was nothing wrong with living in a hotel, but she'd been feeling restless lately. She'd thought it was residual apprehension about Dominique who, according to Cain Casey, had vanished after her funds had disappeared, likely on the run from her business partner, Petrov. But it had been several weeks and she hadn't surfaced, and Royal doubted she would think to look for them here if she was inclined to look for them at all. After a day of mulling it over, she came to the realization it wasn't the fact they were living in a hotel that bothered her, it was that she wasn't entirely sure what the future held, and for the first time in her life, she wanted that kind of clarity. She kept thinking it would come up naturally, but it was easy not to think about the future when they were living their present in paradise.

Later that evening, she asked Siobhan to join her for a walk on the beach. They walked about a quarter mile before she summoned the courage to broach the subject in a roundabout fashion. "I've been thinking about what Ryan said this morning. Would you rather live in a house than a hotel room?"

Siobhan wrapped her arms around Royal's waist. "All I

want is to be where you are. The rest is only window dressing."

She frowned. "Is everything okay?"

Royal smiled. "Of course." She gestured to the ocean. "How could it not be? It's just…"

"You want more."

"Do you?"

Siobhan sighed. "Yes, but sometimes I feel like I'm tempting fate. Happily ever afters don't run in my family."

"Yeah, mine either."

"But happy for now doesn't feel like it's enough." Siobhan tugged her closer. "Not with you. Not for us."

Royal cleared her throat and took the plunge. "Look, I know we have money and security and we're in this gorgeous paradise, but I want the whole package. I want to go to bed with you every night and wake up with you every morning. I want to make a family of our own, and I promise I'll be a better parent than mine were, and I swear I'll love you every day for the rest of my life, and you can stop me now if this isn't what you want because I've been holding this inside since the moment we stepped off that plane, probably longer, and—"

"Me too."

Royal cocked her head. "Sorry, I was on a roll and I'm not sure I heard that."

"I want all of those things. With you. Forever you. I love you, Royal Scott. Let's make a life together."

Royal took both Siobhan's hands in her own. "Yes. A hundred percent. Yes."

About the Author

Carsen Taite's goal as an author is to spin tales with plot lines as interesting as the cases she encountered in her career as a criminal defense lawyer. She is the award-winning author of over twenty novels of romance and romantic intrigue, including the Luca Bennett Bounty Hunter series, the Lone Star Law series, the Legal Affairs romances, and the upcoming Courting Danger series.

Books Available From Bold Strokes Books

A Turn of Fate by Ronica Black. Will Nev and Kinsley finally face their painful past and relent to their powerful, forbidden attraction? Or will facing their past be too much to fight through? (978-1-63555-930-9)

Desires After Dark by MJ Williamz. When her human lover falls deathly ill, Alex, a vampire, must decide which is worse, letting her go or condemning her to everlasting life. (978-1-63555-940-8)

Her Consigliere by Carsen Taite. FBI agent Royal Scott swore an oath to uphold the law, and criminal defense attorney Siobhan Collins pledged her loyalty to the only family she's ever known, but will their love be stronger than the bonds they've vowed to others, or will their competing allegiances tear them apart? (978-1-63555-924-8)

In Our Words: Queer Stories from Black, Indigenous, and People of Color Writers. Stories Selected by Anne Shade and Edited by Victoria Villaseñor. Comprising both the renowned and emerging voices of Black, Indigenous, and People of Color authors, this thoughtfully curated collection of short stories explores the intersection of racial and queer identity. (978-1-63555-936-1)

Measure of Devotion by CF Frizzell. Disguised as her late twin brother, Catherine Samson enters the Civil War to defend the Constitution as a Union soldier, never expecting her life to be altered by a Gettysburg farmer's daughter. (978-1-63555-951-4)

Not Guilty by Brit Ryder. Claire Weaver and Emery Pearson's day jobs clash, even as their desire for each other burns, and a discreet sex-only arrangement is the only option. (978-1-63555-896-8)

Opposites Attract: Butch/Femme Romances by Meghan O'Brien, Aurora Rey & Angie Williams. Sometimes opposites really do attract. Fall in love with these butch/femme romance novellas. (978-1-63555-784-8)

Swift Vengeance by Jean Copeland, Jackie D & Erin Zak. A journalist becomes the subject of her own investigation when sudden strange, violent visions summon her to a summer retreat and into the arms of a killer's possible next victim. (978-1-63555-880-7)

Under Her Influence by Amanda Radley. On their path to #truelove, will Beth and Jemma discover that reality is even better than illusion? (978-1-63555-963-7)

Wasteland by Kristin Keppler & Allisa Bahney. Danielle Clark is fighting against the National Armed Forces and finds peace as a scavenger, until the NAF general's daughter, Katelyn Turner, shows up on her doorstep and brings the fight right back to her. (978-1-63555-935-4)

When In Doubt by VK Powell. Police officer Jeri Wylder thinks she committed a crime in the line of duty but can't remember, until details emerge pointing to a cover-up by those close to her. (978-1-63555-955-2)

A Woman to Treasure by Ali Vali. An ancient scroll isn't the only treasure Levi Montbard finds as she starts her hunt for the truth—all she has to do is prove to Yasmine Hassani that there's more to her than an adventurous soul. (978-1-63555-890-6)

Before. After. Always. by Morgan Lee Miller. Still reeling from her tragic past, Eliza Walsh has sworn off taking risks, until Blake Navarro turns her world right-side up, making her question if falling in love again is worth it. (978-1-63555-845-6)

Bet the Farm by Fiona Riley. Lauren Calloway's luxury real estate sale of the century comes to a screeching halt when dairy farm heiress, and one-night stand, Thea Boudreaux calls her bluff. (978-1-63555-731-2)

Cowgirl by Nance Sparks. The last thing Aren expects is to fall for Carol. Sharing her home is one thing, but sharing her heart means sharing the demons in her past and risking everything to keep Carol safe. (978-1-63555-877-7)

Give In to Me by Elle Spencer. Gabriela Talbot never expected to sleep with her favorite author—certainly not after the scathing review she'd given Whitney Ainsworth's latest book. (978-1-63555-910-1)

Hidden Dreams by Shelley Thrasher. A lethal virus and its resulting vision send Texan Barbara Allan and her lovely guide, Dara, on a journey up Cambodia's Mekong River in search of Barbara's mother's mystifying past. (978-1-63555-856-2)

In the Spotlight by Lesley Davis. For actresses Cole Calder and Eris Whyte, their chance at love runs out fast when a fan's adoration turns to obsession. (978-1-63555-926-2)

Origins by Jen Jensen. Jamis Bachman is pulled into a dangerous mystery that becomes personal when she learns the truth of her origins as a ghost hunter. (978-1-63555-837-1)

Unrivaled by Radclyffe. Zoey Cohen will never accept second place in matters of the heart, even when her rival is a career, and Declan Black has nothing left to give of herself or her heart. (978-1-63679-013-8)

A Fae Tale by Genevieve McCluer. Dovana comes to terms with her changing feelings for her lifelong best friend and fae, Roze. (978-1-63555-918-7)

Accidental Desperados by Lee Lynch. Life is clobbering Berry, Jaudon, and their long romance. The arrival of directionless baby dyke MJ doesn't help. Can they find their passion again—and keep it? (978-1-63555-482-3)

Always Believe by Aimée. Greyson Walsden is pursuing ordination as an Anglican priest. Angela Arlingham doesn't believe in God. Do they follow their vocation or their hearts? (978-1-63555-912-5)

Courage by Jesse J. Thoma. No matter how often Natasha Parsons and Tommy Finch clash on the job, an undeniable attraction simmers just beneath the surface. Can they find the courage to change so love has room to grow? (978-1-63555-802-9)

I Am Chris by R Kent. There's one saving grace to losing everything and moving away. Nobody knows her as Chrissy Taylor. Now Chris can live who he truly is. (978-1-63555-904-0)

The Princess and the Odium by Sam Ledel. Jastyn and Princess Aurelia return to Venostes and join their families in a battle against the dark force to take back their homeland for a chance at a better tomorrow. (978-1-63555-894-4)

The Queen Has a Cold by Jane Kolven. What happens when the heir to the throne isn't a prince or a princess? (978-1-63555-878-4)